N

THE MAID AND THE MANSION:

A SCANDALOUS DEATH

(The Maid and the Mansion Cozy Mystery—Book Two)

FIONA GRACE

Fiona Grace

Fiona Grace is author of the LACEY DOYLE COZY MYSTERY series, comprising nine books; of the TUSCAN VINEYARD COZY MYSTERY series, comprising seven books; of the DUBIOUS WITCH COZY MYSTERY series, comprising three books; of the BEACHFRONT BAKERY COZY MYSTERY series, comprising six books; of the CATS AND DOGS COZY MYSTERY series, comprising nine books; of the ELIZA MONTAGU COZY MYSTERY series, comprising nine books (and counting); of the ENDLESS HARBOR ROMANTIC COMEDY series, comprising nine books (and counting); of the INN AT DUNE ISLAND ROMANTIC COMEDY series, comprising five books (and counting); of the INN BY THE SEA ROMANTIC COMEDY series, comprising five books (and counting); and of the MAID AND THE MANSION COZY MYSTERY series, comprising five books (and counting).

Fiona would love to hear from you, so please visit www.fionagraceauthor.com to receive free ebooks, hear the latest news, and stay in touch.

ISBN: 978-1-0943-8389-7

BOOKS BY FIONA GRACE

THE MAID AND THE MANSION COZY MYSTERY
A MYSTERIOUS MURDER (Book #1)
A SCANDALOUS DEATH (Book #2)
A MISSING GUEST (Book #3)
AN UNSOLVABLE CRIME (Book #4)
AN IMPOSSIBLE HEIST (Book #5)

INN BY THE SEA ROMANTIC COMEDY
A NEW LOVE (Book #1)
A NEW CHANCE (Book #2)
A NEW HOME (Book #3)
A NEW LIFE (Book #4)
A NEW ME (Book #5)

THE INN AT DUNE ISLAND ROMANTIC COMEDY
A CHANCE LOVE (Book #1)
A CHANCE FALL (Book #2)
A CHANCE ROMANCE (Book #3)
A CHANCE CHRISTMAS (Book #4)
A CHANCE ENGAGEMENT (Book #5)

ENDLESS HARBOR ROMANTIC COMEDY
ALWAYS, WITH YOU (Book #1)
ALWAYS, FOREVER (Book #2)
ALWAYS, PLUS ONE (Book #3)
ALWAYS, TOGETHER (Book #4)
ALWAYS, LIKE THIS (Book #5)
ALWAYS, FATED (Book #6)
ALWAYS, FOR LOVE (Book #7)
ALWAYS, JUST US (Book #8)
ALWAYS, IN LOVE (Book #9)

ELIZA MONTAGU COZY MYSTERY
MURDER AT THE HEDGEROW (Book #1)
A DALLOP OF DEATH (Book #2)

CALAMITY AT THE BALL (Book #3)
A SPEAKEASY DEMISE (Book #4)
A FLAPPER FATALITY (Book #5)
BUMPED BY A DAME (Book #6)
A DOLL'S DEBACLE (Book #7)
A FELLA'S RUIN (Book #8)
A GAL'S OFFING (Book #9)

LACEY DOYLE COZY MYSTERY
MURDER IN THE MANOR (Book#1)
DEATH AND A DOG (Book #2)
CRIME IN THE CAFE (Book #3)
VEXED ON A VISIT (Book #4)
KILLED WITH A KISS (Book #5)
PERISHED BY A PAINTING (Book #6)
SILENCED BY A SPELL (Book #7)
FRAMED BY A FORGERY (Book #8)
CATASTROPHE IN A CLOISTER (Book #9)

TUSCAN VINEYARD COZY MYSTERY
AGED FOR MURDER (Book #1)
AGED FOR DEATH (Book #2)
AGED FOR MAYHEM (Book #3)
AGED FOR SEDUCTION (Book #4)
AGED FOR VENGEANCE (Book #5)
AGED FOR ACRIMONY (Book #6)
AGED FOR MALICE (Book #7)

DUBIOUS WITCH COZY MYSTERY
SKEPTIC IN SALEM: AN EPISODE OF MURDER (Book #1)
SKEPTIC IN SALEM: AN EPISODE OF CRIME (Book #2)
SKEPTIC IN SALEM: AN EPISODE OF DEATH (Book #3)

BEACHFRONT BAKERY COZY MYSTERY
BEACHFRONT BAKERY: A KILLER CUPCAKE (Book #1)
BEACHFRONT BAKERY: A MURDEROUS MACARON (Book #2)
BEACHFRONT BAKERY: A PERILOUS CAKE POP (Book #3)
BEACHFRONT BAKERY: A DEADLY DANISH (Book #4)
BEACHFRONT BAKERY: A TREACHEROUS TART (Book #5)
BEACHFRONT BAKERY: A CALAMITOUS COOKIE (Book #6)

CATS AND DOGS COZY MYSTERY

A VILLA IN SICILY: OLIVE OIL AND MURDER (Book #1)
A VILLA IN SICILY: FIGS AND A CADAVER (Book #2)
A VILLA IN SICILY: VINO AND DEATH (Book #3)
A VILLA IN SICILY: CAPERS AND CALAMITY (Book #4)
A VILLA IN SICILY: ORANGE GROVES AND VENGEANCE (Book #5)
A VILLA IN SICILY: CANNOLI AND A CASUALTY (Book #6)

CHAPTER ONE

"Mary!" The querulous voice resounded down the corridor from the grand bedroom suite beyond. "Is that you? I called you up because I need you here immediately! I have a catastrophe on my hands!"

"On my way, my lady!" Politely, Mary Adams called back as she hurried up the wide spiral staircase, in a voice that she hoped was loud enough to be heard by Lady Middlefield, but not loud enough to be construed as rude.

She'd been in her small upstairs bedroom, about to start her day's work, when the buzzer had summoned her to Lady Middlefield's suite, and she'd quickly pulled on her shoes and rushed to help.

Even though 'hurry' meant exactly that, she stopped for a moment at the top of the stairs to tug her apron straight, brush a speck of dust off her dark blue dress, and make sure that no unruly locks of butter blond hair were peeking out of her lacy white cap.

A month of working at Middlefield Manor had taught her that the widowed matriarch who oversaw the entire estate, was somewhat persnickety.

Maybe 'focused on detail' would be a kinder word to use, Mary decided, as she hurried into the opulent bedroom. She'd always been a person who believed in making allowances for the elderly. As her mum had always reminded her, growing older was a privilege denied to many, but it often meant putting up with a lot more aches, pains, and general irritation with life.

She guessed that was true, even for an immensely wealthy woman approaching her seventy-fifth birthday, whose husband had passed away a few years ago, and whose word was law, across the entire estate.

Now, what was this catastrophe?

After a month's work experience as a housemaid in the stately home of Middlefield Manor, Mary was guessing it might be that the lady had mislaid another piece of her jewelry – perhaps one of her diamond earrings, and was looking for the first available person to hunt for it.

Last week, a missing necklace had resulted in her entire suite being turned upside down – and with the necklace still not found, Mary was wondering if the elderly lady herself had absentmindedly hidden it away somewhere.

Lady Middlefield's bedroom was on the mansion's second floor, with a view over the rose gardens. Now, going into winter, they were nothing more than neatly pruned stubs, but she was sure that in summertime, they would be a glorious kaleidoscope of color.

Rain was spattering the window as she headed across the expanse of royal blue carpet and over to the small card table where a tea tray had been placed. From the rows of playing cards that were laid out, Lady Middlefield appeared to have been busy with a game of patience – but was now tapping the table with a distinct lack of patience, waiting for Mary to approach.

With her cloud of well-styled gray hair, her sharp nose, and her piercing voice, Lady Middlefield seemed to pick up on every little detail when it came to her servants, and how they did their jobs.

Plus – unusually for an elderly, upper-class lady, she remembered the names of every staff member. In fact, Mary decided she could probably identify people by their footfalls alone. Cleaning her rooms was the most challenging part of her housemaid's job so far.

Working in a factory, as Mary had done up until a month ago when all the men had begun returning from the war, was actually less demanding than this.

At least there was only one place for a bolt to go – in its rightful spot on the engine.

But when it came to Lady Middlefield's possessions, there were at least three places for everything to go, and they depended on the weather, the schedule for the day, as well as the lady's mood.

She might want her pearl gray velvet gloves to be put away in the glove drawer in her dressing room. Or else, she might want them to be placed on her dressing table ready for her to wear – but sometimes, having them on the card table seemed to be her preference. But again, she might have identified an invisible smudge or dirty mark on one of the gloves which meant that even the sight of them offended her eyes, and the gloves were to be instantly sent down the laundry chute.

It was all very peculiar, and Mary had to admit, she hadn't yet gotten the hang of it.

"Good morning, my lady," she said politely.

"I've spilled my tea!" Lady Middlefield said, with a fractious note to her voice. "Clean it up, would you, Mary?"

So that was the catastrophe? Well, everyone had different definitions of the word.

Now, where was the spilled tea? It must be that tiny dot of liquid there, between the three of hearts and the queen of spades. The cup itself, a fine china item with pink roses around the outside, was set neatly down in its saucer.

"If you'll excuse me?" She rummaged in her cleaning bucket and produced a cloth, with which she dabbed at the minuscule mark.

"It has probably ruined the polished surface!" the lady lamented. "You'll need to come back and shine it later on. Maybe this afternoon."

"I'll do that, my lady," Mary promised, making a mental note to fit in this chore between her usual Tuesday job of cleaning the parlor, and today's special task of stripping down and cleaning the guest bedrooms. There was a small birthday celebration for Lady Middlefield at the manor house tonight, and guests were arriving later.

"Just be sure that I am in this room when you do the work," the lady said sharply. "Or else, my assistant must be here. I still haven't found out what happened to that missing ornamental elephant that disappeared in October!"

"I will make sure, my lady," Mary said politely.

It was a source of great intrigue to her that Lady Middlefield would not allow any of the housemaids to be in her bedroom unless she herself was present, or else, her attendant was working in the small annex room just outside the bedroom door.

Did she think somebody was going to steal something? The reference to the elephant hinted at that, but Mary had also noticed that the elderly lady was extremely protective about the small chest by the side of her four-poster bed. Once, by mistake, Mary had actually put a hand on that chest's wide, domed lid, thinking that because of its location within the room, it contained spare linen.

The screech of, "Don't touch that!" from Lady Middlefield, as she spun around from her card table, had nearly shattered her eardrums. Of course, ever since then, Mary had desperately wondered what was in that chest. Even now, she had to exercise a good deal of self-control to stop herself from glancing at it curiously.

She forced herself not to. It wasn't her business to be curious, it was her business to do her housemaid's job to the best of her ability.

After all, as a twenty-three year old from the working classes, with no close family left alive in the world, and no qualifications or money to her name, she was lucky to have this job. Especially since it was a relatively well paying one, in the countryside, with board and accommodation as part of the package. In these tough post-war times, there were a lot of people without the luxury of a job at all.

And especially after what had happened at her previous place of employment, Coldstream Lodge, Mary felt grateful to be here.

She stepped aside, deftly tweaking the cleaning cloth away, and doing her best to resume her normal state of invisibility, which she had discovered that most servants possessed automatically in the eyes of the upper classes.

But it was almost as if she and Lady Middlefield had shared a weird psychic moment there when thinking about her past.

Because, as she turned away to tidy Lady Middlefield's shoe cupboard, she felt the grand dame's eyes on her. But that gaze was as nothing compared to the question that followed.

"You know, Mary," she said thoughtfully. "I heard from a guest who dropped by yesterday that there was some trouble at your previous workplace. Is that correct? Because I was never made aware of those facts when you arrived here!"

CHAPTER TWO

Mary felt her heart stop beating for a moment, and then accelerate in a volley of thuds that she was sure might be visible from under the frilly, full length apron she wore.

Of course, there had been trouble – and it had been bad. She hadn't caused it and had been totally innocent of it, but that wasn't what the police had believed for a while.

For a day and a half that felt like the longest of her life, she'd been accused of the terrible crime of murder, and had gone to great efforts to clear her own name.

She'd never thought that the details would travel this far, especially since Middlefield Manor was well over a hundred miles away from Coldstream Lodge. It was in an entirely different county, all the way in the northeast of England's Midlands.

After the 'trouble', such as it was, had been resolved, and she'd helped the police find the real killer, she and her best friend had been exchanged for another servant in a swap. These exchanges of staff happened regularly, Mary was surprised to learn, even between estate owners who didn't know each other particularly well. Coldstream Lodge had required a second cook, Middlefield Manor had one cook too many but needed housemaids, and so the word had gone out, and a trade had been done.

That was the official story, anyway. After the 'trouble' was resolved, she suspected the real reason for the trade had been so that the team at Coldstream Lodge could start afresh after the murder, without her there.

Mary had been an unwanted reminder to them of that stressful time, and so they'd sent her elsewhere. Luckily, because two housemaids had been required, Hannah had come along with her.

And now, somehow, Lady Middlefield was ignoring the fact that 'Two Reliable and Honest Maids', had been sent – she'd seen the note that had accompanied Hannah and herself – and asking these very dangerous questions.

Better to be truthful, she decided. Telling a lie could come back to bite her. Lady Middlefield was clearly a person of vast experience thanks to her senior years, and maybe that would mean she understood the situation if Mary could explain it properly.

"Yes, there was some trouble there," she said. "I actually played a small part in helping solve a difficult situation."

"Did you know?" Lady Middlefield quirked a finely drawn eyebrow. "And how exactly did you do that?"

Was her voice curious? Was this just a chance to catch up with the non-local gossip? How many details should she give out?

Perhaps this was a chance for her to speak well of her skills, while avoiding any troubling details.

"I had a knack for problem solving, and was able to put together a few facts to help the police," she said.

Instantly, Lady Middlefield's eyebrows raised skywards.

"The police?" she echoed. "It seems you are keeping secrets from me, Mary Adams. And I do not allow secrets at Middlefield Manor!" The stern note in her voice was audible.

Oh, no! So Lady Middlefield hadn't known the police were involved? And now this had come as a shock to her?

Dithering frantically about what to say next, as her brain raced, Mary was saved by the arrival of quick footsteps from the corridor.

It was exactly nine a.m. – the chime of the grandfather clock on the landing confirmed it – and that meant Lady Middlefield's assistant, Howard, had arrived on duty.

"Good morning, my lady!"

Resplendent in a tweed waistcoat and trousers, with his brown hair neatly parted on the side, Howard was excessively friendly to his employer, Lady Middlefield, while managing to behave in a distinctly cooler way to everyone else.

Therefore, Mary wasn't surprised when he frowned at her from beneath his well-groomed brown eyebrows.

"Are you all done in here?" he asked her, not addressing her by name – if he did know it, he wasn't choosing to use it. "Because I need to revise some ledger details with my lady, relating to the manor's winter expenses, before the breakfast tray arrives."

"I'll speak to you later, young lady," Lady Middlefield warned in tones that told Mary very clearly that the gray-haired lady might be elderly, but she was by no means forgetful.

Mary thought uneasily that it felt as if she had a sharply pointed sword hanging over her now, as she hastened out of the lady's rooms.

Letting out a sigh of relief, she and her cleaning bucket headed down the stairs, and as she did, she saw her best friend Hannah, coming up.

"Mary!" Hannah took advantage of the fact there was nobody around, to adjust her own frilly cap, which was very loose, and causing her bobbing brown curls to spill out onto her shoulders. Quickly, Mary moved forward to help her tuck her recalcitrant hair under the cap. She pushed up the last stray lock as Hannah gave a grateful sigh.

"Thank you. I was out in the wind just now, taking some blankets across to the coach house, and it blasted this cap right off my head! I had to run after it," Hannah muttered, in tones that were low enough to not possibly be overheard from upstairs.

"If Lady Middlefield had been looking out of the window and seen you chasing your cap, she'd have been furious!" Mary whispered, and they both snorted with hastily suppressed laughter.

"I was coming to find you, because Lord Edward wants the three guest bedrooms prepared now. He says it's likely that at least one of the new guests will be arriving this morning, and not this afternoon. I believe they're trying to get here before an early winter storm arrives."

As if on cue, another gust of wind caused the panes in the staircase window to rattle. Glad she wasn't out in that icy gale, Mary shivered.

"Let's go and get it done quick, then. We'd better add some extra wood supplies to those fireplaces."

Glad to have the chance to work alongside her friend – and the one person at Middlefield Manor who did know exactly what trouble she'd been caught up in – Mary rushed down the corridor to the scullery, replenished her cleaning supplies, and headed off up the back staircase that was a shortcut to the guest rooms on the manor's third floor.

"Is Lord Colin in a good mood today?" Mary asked.

"Is he ever in a good mood?" Hannah replied, sounding genuinely puzzled by the question.

Lord Colin, who was Lady Middlefield's oldest son, was a man in his mid-forties, with a thick head of dark hair threaded with silver, a passion for his horses, and a mercurial temper. It always felt as if you were treading a tightrope when you spoke to Lord Colin. The wrong answer could easily result in a death-defying plunge off it. And Mary hadn't yet worked out what seemed to trigger these outbursts.

Luckily, she hadn't had too much to do with him so far, but as they rushed through the winding corridors, she heard his voice from beyond one of the doors. It seemed that two of the footmen were the target of his wrath today.

"Jenson and Foulds, I thought I asked you both to make sure the two top storage sheds were cleared! I've just been in there and there are still some old buckets lying around, and a load of wood. Our esteemed guests are going to want to park inside with this storm approaching! I don't want shoddy work from you. This is urgent. We're all doing different tasks today, preparing for this birthday celebration, but that doesn't mean the tasks don't get done correctly! We don't want any trouble arising due to your incompetence!"

"Sorry, Lord Colin," Jenson's voice could be clearly heard through the doorway as they rushed past.

She hoped that the manor house wasn't heading into troubled waters with the arrival of these guests. After what had happened at Coldstream Lodge, Mary was very eager to avoid trouble at all costs.

At that point, the corridor made a left turn, and Lord Colin's angry diatribe was no longer audible.

Another branch of the passage led her to the guest rooms, which were located on a wide corridor in the lodge's east wing.

With her buckets clattering as she walked, and Hannah marching along behind her half buried under a massive pile of fresh towels, blankets and sheets, they entered the first room.

There, Lady Ella, who was Lord Colin's wife, was busy directing one of the other maids.

"Yes, we'll need to get fresh flowers in this room. Hopefully you can find some in the conservatory? Even if it's just some greenery, it's always nice and welcoming to have flowers on a guest's arrival, I think."

She was as sweet and friendly as Lord Edward was tempestuous – a calm faced woman with pale blond hair that she wore in a braided style, pinned on top of her head. Having given her instructions, she hurried out, checking her notepad as she walked, and muttering to herself, "Now, where's the housekeeper going to be right now?"

Mary was glad to see that the housemaid she was addressing, who'd been told to get the greenery, was one of the maids that she enjoyed working with.

Sarah-Jane was in her late thirties, and had a cheerful, round face with pink cheeks that flushed easily, chestnut hair, and a jovial laugh. She always used to clap her hand over her mouth when she laughed, as if she was nervous that she'd cause too much of a commotion with the raucous sound.

"Hello, Hannah and Mary," she said.

"Hello, Sarah-Jane."

"Flowers and greenery!" She rolled her eyes. "Flowers, at this time? I was in the conservatory yesterday and there's nothing much growing, even there. I think I'll have to pick a couple of pine branches if greenery's what she wants!"

"How about an arrangement of pine cones and pine needles?" Mary suggested, her imagination immediately veering in the direction of Christmas, which wasn't too far away. "Some holly? Some mistletoe?"

"Oooh, but we don't want the guests to get any ideas and go kissing each other under it," Sarah-Jane said, her merry brown eyes sparkling as she let out her trademark guffaw. "But yes, I think that pine cone and pine needle arrangement might work. I'd better go and forage for them before the rain comes. Or maybe it'll be snow," she said, bustling out.

Mary got to work with her bucket, towels and mop, cleaning every inch of the room's floor and paying special attention to the areas where she'd noticed that Lady Ella liked to check. She had a habit of running her hand over the top shelf of a bookcase and then checking her finger for dust.

Only the top shelf. None of the other shelves. All the same, Mary always tried her best to clean every shelf the same, because you never knew.

Working quickly, because if guests were outrunning the storm, they might arrive at any moment, Mary cleaned the rooms, scrubbing the floors, polishing the bed railings, making sure that all the wooden furniture – the chair, the desk, the dressing table – gleamed with a spotless shine. She plumped the cushions on the beds once Hannah had finished making them, and then made sure that the cushions of the armchairs were all dust free.

Somewhere during her whirl around the three bedrooms – the Blue Room, the Green Room and the Ivory Room – Sarah-Jane reappeared, with vases containing fragrant branches of pine and holly, with some pine cones, that she arranged on the desks.

"Those really do work well." Finally reaching the end of her flurry of cleaning, Mary stood back, flanked by Sarah-Jane and Hannah, admiring the look of the final room – the Green Room.

"They smell so lovely and piney," Hannah said. "It's as if the woods came right here into the room!"

"Yes, and they look welcoming, like a cottage in the forest," Mary said. "Although I'm sure Lady Middlefield wouldn't like the Green Room referred to as a cottage."

"You're right," Sarah-Jane giggled.

"Does Lady Middlefield like anything?" Hannah whispered. "She seems very disapproving, a lot of the time."

"She is," Mary admitted. "But people get crotchety with age. That's what my mum always used to say."

She turned away from the Green Room and headed for the service corridor, wanting to get her cleaning equipment well out of the way before any guests arrived. Working as a maid, she'd quickly learned that people wanted squeaky clean rooms, but nobody wanted to see any evidence of cleaning. She remembered how Lady Middlefield had reacted when Mary had accidentally left a feather duster in a visible position while she'd been cleaning the bathroom.

"What... is... *that*?" she'd said, staring at it in a shocked way as if it was a huge hairy spider, and not an innocent piece of cleaning equipment.

So, as fast as possible, she whisked her mop, bucket, broom and cloths out of the main corridor and into a side corridor.

There, she hurried along, needing to get to her next chore as fast as possible, with all the pressure of this birthday celebration weighing on her mind.

Just as she emerged from the service corridor, she heard an angry voice and fast footsteps approaching from the opposite side of the manor.

And this voice belonged to the tempestuous and grumpy Colin Middlefield. Not a person she wanted to meet while laden down with cleaning equipment and walking along one of the lodge's main corridors.

Quickly, Mary ducked back through the archway and pressed herself against the wall.

The voices approached. Colin Middlefield and one other, that uttered no more than a grunt. But as they reached her, she realized this wasn't just an argument, but something more serious.

"If you tell a soul about this, I'll make sure you face the consequences," Lord Colin threatened.

And then the footsteps stopped – right by the archway where she was standing, pressed against the wall, but visible if either of the men looked her way.

CHAPTER THREE

"What do you mean, I'll face the consequences?" Mary flattened herself even further against the wall as Colin Middlefield, clearly enraged by what the other man was saying, lashed back at him. Now she recognized the voice. It was Warwick Middlefield, the youngest of the three brothers, and this was the first time she'd heard the usually drunken Warwick sound even remotely sober. "You're the one who – who was responsible for this whole situation existing at all!"

"Me? You're blaming me for all of this?"

"Yes, I am! Everything was fine, until you..." Warwick's voice dropped to a mumble as Mary tried her best not to breathe.

"That was not my doing!" Colin protested, also in a mumble, sounding as if he was getting the words out through gritted teeth. "And just shut up about it now. If you blab, Mother will find out."

It seemed that this birthday party was bringing out the worst in everyone, Mary thought, trying her best to keep out of sight until, thankfully, the footsteps started up again and the two arguing men headed out of her earshot.

Then, she let out a deep breath, deciding it was safe to walk out of the service corridor again, and down the main corridor, taking the branch that led to the kitchen and scullery.

What had that argument been about, she wondered. She knew Warwick was the family's drunken rebel, and Colin was the one who tried to run everything – but he seemed to do so badly, because he was so erratic and tempestuous.

The middle brother, Martin, she seldom saw. He'd apparently been in a riding accident two years ago, requiring a lengthy stay in bed to fix multiple broken bones. But now that all his bones were better, he seemed to be permanently sickly with stomach problems. She'd brought him tea once, when the usual housemaid had been off duty. Looking pale and ill, propped up on his pillows, he'd thanked her in a low voice.

Behind the scullery was the servants' pantry, and as Mary replaced the bucket and mop on the shelf, the troubling thoughts of the Middlefield brothers went out of her mind as her nose twitched.

The smells coming from that room were utterly delightful, and since she'd been at work since seven a.m., she was already starving.

She peeked in through the door, seeing that the only other occupant of the room was Hannah, who had cut a few slices of the steaming nut and seed loaf that the cook had brought straight out of the oven.

"Bread!"

Mary was drawn straight in by that enticing aroma.

The crusty, sweet smell of bread, and the delightfully tangy hint of the raisins and sultanas that nestled inside its warm crumb, were enough to get her mouth watering.

"Cook has added flaked hazelnuts, and a few cranberries," Hannah said. "Here's the butter."

Her friend kindly poured her a cup of tea while Mary buttered herself two thick slices of bread. The butter was melting on top, and oozing into the crumb, because the bread was still so deliciously hot.

"Only a few more hours to go until the birthday party. And then, hopefully, we'll get a day off," Hannah said, as Mary bit into her bread, washing it down with a mouthful of sweet tea.

"We're only a few miles from the sea here," Mary said. "I don't know the exact distance, but when that easterly wind blows, I can smell the sea on it, just as if it was over the next hill."

The sea! It sounded so incredibly romantic. All her life she'd wanted to go to the seaside. Winter wasn't the best time, of course, because it would be far too cold to do as much as dabble her toes in the water, but imagine seeing the crashing waves? The expanse of ocean? Hearing the sound of the breakers on the beach and feeling the spray on her face? What an amazing sight that would be.

"Yes. Fifteen miles away, apparently," Hannah said. "That's where the town of Skegness is, anyway, and one of the other maids was telling me yesterday that it has a wonderful beach. Miles long and sandy, not like so many of the pebble beaches in this country!"

"A sandy beach?" Imagine going for a walk on it, and taking off her shoes, no matter how cold the weather, and feeling the sand in between her toes? "I think we must go for an outing, don't you?"

"I hope we can get a day off together." Hannah cut herself a sneaky third slice of the bread. "I don't know if Mrs. Inglethorpe will allow it, though."

The head housekeeper's beaky nose and piercing eyes came immediately to Mary's mind. She was a very strict woman, and woe betide anyone who was late for their shift or skimped on their work.

"Well, it can't hurt to ask," Mary said. "Sometimes, bosses just don't think about things, but don't really mind when they get done. I remember when I worked at the factory, there was no hot tea available in the building. You had to walk all the way to the upper building, which took a good ten minutes. So I decided I was going to suggest to the owner that he put a kettle in the back room in our building. I told him it would save us a lot of time, and that would mean that we were able to get back to our workstations sooner. And also it would mean less wet, muddy footprints across the floor!"

"That was brave of you, telling him how to run his business," Hannah said, her eyes wide.

"It was scary to do it," Mary admitted. "But he agreed. So it ended up being better for everyone."

"What's your argument going to be for asking Mrs. Inglethorpe if we can take a day off together?" Hannah asked.

"I'll need to think about that," Mary admitted. "Because there aren't as many obvious benefits to her. It's just giving us what we want. But hopefully, we can come up with a convincing argument. Maybe working really hard today will be enough."

She used the last of her bread to mop up a small pool of melted butter. How delicious! There was a lot to be said, she decided, for working in a country house, where such scrumptious food was available at any time, and on the premises.

Different as it was from her factory work, Mary decided she had a lot to be grateful for. Just as long as that birthday party didn't end up upsetting the apple cart. Thanks to this birthday, tensions within the house, that she hadn't even known had existed, were ratcheting up.

And at that moment, a sharp voice coming from the kitchen, called out, "Is there anybody around? Anybody at all? We have guests arriving, and there isn't a footman in sight! Come on, quick, if you're available!"

Pausing only to put her plate neatly in the sink, and wipe her mouth in case any stray crumbs remained, Mary hurried out, with Hannah hot on her heels.

Outside was the head housekeeper whom they'd just been discussing. Mrs. Inglethorpe was wearing a perfectly starched white apron and an annoyed expression. It didn't soften as Mary and Hannah hurried up.

"I don't know why a change to the schedule is a reason for everyone to disappear from duty!" she chastised, as if Mary and

Hannah had been deliberately hiding themselves away and stuffing their faces, instead of taking a short but well earned tea break.

"What can we do to help out?" Mary asked quickly, and now at last, with her irritation off her chest, the head housekeeper's stern expression relented.

"Well, you can go down to where those cars are arriving, and unpack everything that's there. We've had three guests arrive simultaneously!" Mrs. Inglethorpe glanced down at the clipboard that seemed to be an actual part of her, because Mary had never seen her without it, and had a private certainty that she even slept with it.

"The contents of the Bugatti are for the Green Room. The contents of the Bentley are for the Blue Room. And the contents of the black Rolls Royce are for the Ivory Room. Do not, under any circumstances, get the contents mixed up, or our guests will be very annoyed."

"We'll do so right away," Mary said politely, remembering that it was even more important than usual to get into Mrs. Inglethorpe's good books, since she and Hannah now had an aim in mind, and an outing on a mutual day off to hope for.

Turning away, she hurried out, reciting to herself, "Bugatti, Green Room. Bentley, Blue Room. Rolls Royce, Ivory Room." It would be easy to get confused between the three otherwise, especially since the storm was now not just brewing, but descending. The clouds outside looked dark and heavy, and as she rushed out through the front door, a gust of wind almost blew her cap right off her head.

She grabbed it with her hand, clamping it down onto her head with the palm as she hurried to the first car.

There, two stressed-looking butlers were busy unpacking a large suitcase, with the help of a wild-haired chauffeur whose top hat had already flown off in the gale, and was lodged in a nearby hedge.

"We're here to help," Mary said cheerfully, recognizing the closest one. "Good morning, Swindon. Looks like there's some bad weather on the way."

"That there is, Ms. Adams," the butler said. "And the Mersey family has brought everything but the kitchen sink with them, as usual."

That was certainly true. The back of the Bugatti was absolutely crammed with belongings. Top of the pile, in a place of honor, Mary was surprised to see a luxurious looking cage, with a wrought iron door and a large red velvet cushion inside, atop which rested a long haired, regal looking, white cat.

"Oh, what a beauty you are!"

Carefully, Mary lifted the cage. It was surely important to get this cat inside before the storm arrived. She knew that no feline, especially one that seemed so spoiled, would appreciate getting as much as a drop of rain on their fluffy coat.

"That's Snowdon, Lady Mersey's pet," the chauffeur explained. "He travels everywhere with her, and has the run of her manor house when she's home."

Mary didn't know Lady Mersey, but instinctively, she already liked her. What a nice person she must be to take her cat along with her, traveling in such fine style.

It was only as she lifted out the cage that she was in a position to glance over at the car next door, the Bentley.

Just the name of it had already sounded a small, but hopeful, alarm bell in Mary's mind.

While at Coldstream Manor, she'd had a brief encounter with an arriving guest, Gilbert MacLeod. From Mary's side, she had to admit, it had been a huge crush at first sight. Then, when she arrived here at Middlefield Manor, she'd met him again, and he'd mentioned that he was going to be here again in the future.

And this car looked identical to his.

Could Gilbert MacLeod be one of the invited guests, and if so, would she have the chance to speak to him?

Mary felt her face grow hot at the thought. Obviously, there was no way that they could ever be more than friends. After all, he was a wealthy landowner, with parents who owned a huge estate bordering Scotland, and she was nothing more than a humble housemaid, one of the invisible cast of characters within the manor's walls.

But – well, just a short conversation with him last time had left her feeling so happy. Surely that would be possible again?

Reminding herself that she was jumping to conclusions, and that she didn't even know if this was his car or just a similar model, Mary firmly controlled her moment of excitement, and turned to the front door, carrying the cat in his cage with as steady a hand as she could.

She headed inside and up the stairs, turning right and then left. Snowdon seemed to be enjoying the journey. At any rate, he was still curled up on his cushion and appeared relaxed, although his eyes were blinking as he took in his new surroundings.

She headed into the Green Room, where another housemaid was frantically packing clothes out of a large trunk, and into the wardrobe.

“Here is Snowdon,” Mary said, wondering where the cat would feel most at ease. Deciding that he might enjoy a view, she put the cage down on the window seat. He began grooming his tail, clearly at ease with his surroundings, so she hurried back downstairs again, now with Gilbert MacLeod firmly in her mind.

And there he was!

It was him. Tall, dark haired and rangy, wearing that same jacket she remembered from last time, that looked like a shabby old favorite, and not like an ostentatiously new item. He was in conversation with Colin Middlefield, and surprisingly, Colin was talking and laughing, looking more animated than she remembered seeing him so far.

“Yes, we’ve got a couple of new horses for this season,” she heard Colin say as they passed.

“Lady Middlefield has always had an exceptional eye for a horse,” Gilbert said, and Mary found herself flushing at the sound of his pleasant voice, with its slight Scottish accent, and its deep yet cheerful tone.

Of course, she couldn’t go over and greet him. He’d said he was looking forward to seeing her, the last time they’d met, but that might have just been a brief bit of flirtatiousness on his part, or even simple politeness. And Mary knew she could not, under any circumstances, put her job at risk. Flirting with guests, or appearing too forward, would be heavily frowned upon in any stately home, and she knew that if Colin was watching, it would most likely be an instantly dismissable offense.

So there was nothing she could do but walk past, and remember, with a surge of happiness, how lovely their short conversations had been, and how her feelings for him seemed only to have intensified since she’d last seen him.

Imagine if he spoke to her right now? Imagine if he called out, "Hello there, Mary Adams," and she was seen – in the best way possible?

But he didn’t even look her way as he passed by, because he was talking to Colin. Probably, he had a beautiful girlfriend or fiancé by now and had forgotten about her completely. It had, after all, been a month.

Given that, it would probably be wisest for her to stay out of his way completely, she decided. She didn’t want any misunderstandings or embarrassing situations to arise. An uneasy mix of disappointment and relief churned inside her as she headed outside again.

Luckily, it seemed that Gilbert traveled light, and there was nothing left in the Bentley by the time she returned to the driveway. Only the third and final car, the Rolls Royce, remained to be unpacked. Mary picked up a massive armful of spare clothing, including coats, hats, scarves, shawls, and a pair of boots, which she just managed to snag by their laces.

Carrying all of this, somewhat blindly thanks to the towering mass of clothes, she headed back inside. More by feel than by sight, she threaded her way into the service corridors, climbed the stairs, and went into the Ivory Room. After putting all the clothes down on the four poster bed, with its spotless ivory coverlet, she then unpacked them all into the large mahogany wardrobe, and the chest of drawers beside it with its shiny brass handles.

Then, with that chore done, she left the room quickly, so that it would appear to the arriving guests as if it had all been unpacked and put away by magic.

Except, as she passed the Blue Room, keeping her face firmly turned away just in case, she heard a familiar voice, that halted her in her tracks.

"Mary! Mary Adams. Is that you?"

CHAPTER FOUR

By the time Mary had whirled around to stare into the Blue Room, she was already blushing like a tomato.

And there was Gilbert, sitting on the bed and lacing up a pair of sturdy-looking boots.

She took him in, her heart pounding. Those freckles on his nose and cheeks, the quirk to his mouth that made him look as if he took the world a little less seriously than most. His dark, wayward hair that waved across his forehead. The expression in his dark blue eyes as he took her in.

"Mr. MacLeod," she said. "How nice to see you here."

"I feel terrible for not having greeted you earlier," he said. "I was looking out for you, and thought I saw you as you passed, but then I wasn't sure – your hair was all covered up in that cap. Only when I looked around did I see one of those golden locks peeking out," he said with a smile.

Her pleasure at him having noticed her hair was briefly overshadowed by the fact that some of it was showing under her work cap, which would trigger Lady Middlefield's intense disapproval. She raised a hand and tried to tuck the lock away while answering him politely.

"I remember you said you'd be visiting again. Are you here for Lady Middlefield's birthday?"

"I'm actually not here for the birthday," he explained. "I'm probably the only guest who isn't. I'm here to talk to Colin Middlefield. We're looking at starting up a new venture, some hybrid seeds that promise a much healthier yield of wheat. He has several wheat fields that he said he might plant on an experimental basis. So, I'm here to plant the seeds for that, and it just so happened that my visit coincided with this big birthday."

"The seeds of the idea?" she asked, with a flicker of amusement.

"Exactly," he said, and now his mouth quirked all the way up into that smile that made her feel ready to melt.

"But tell me," he added, "are you enjoying working here? Are you happy, are you making friends?"

"I am," Mary said. "It's a well run household and the people are all – well, interesting," she said. "Most of them are very nice. Lady Middlefield is rather awe-inspiring. I've made good friends with the other housemaids," she said, thinking of Sarah-Jane and her rollicking laugh.

"Lady Middlefield is a grand dame of note," Gilbert agreed. "Colin was telling me that even though she doesn't play an active part in running the household, she still insists on inspecting all the ledgers, every quarter."

"Yes. She really manages the household with a forceful hand," Mary said, wondering as she spoke whether 'forceful' was the right word, or whether it was too strong. "She gets help from her assistant, Howard, but he's just there to do what she tells him to." She wrinkled her nose, remembering Howard's snobbish demeanor, and the irritating habit he had of being obsequiously pleasant to Lady Middlefield and nobody else.

She had the impression that Gilbert wanted to ask her more. That he'd hoped to find out more about how she was personally enjoying it here. So, she added in more detail. "I'm working with my good friend, Hannah, who moved with me from Coldstream Lodge."

"And-" He was about to ask something else, but then stopped himself and shook his head. He looked rather embarrassed, in fact. Mary suddenly wondered if he'd been planning to ask her if she'd met anybody – if she had a fella in her life. It seemed like a wild theory, but there had been something in his tone that had hinted toward it when he'd asked that question.

"How about you?" she asked. "Are you still traveling a lot?"

"Yes, a lot, particularly seeing it's now the winter months. Normally I travel more in summer, and then spend winter freezing in our rather cold manor house." He sighed. "You know, we've lived there for eight years so far, but has there been an opportunity to upgrade the fireplaces? It seems my father always has more important things to think about."

That was interesting to Mary. She'd assumed that Gilbert would have grown up in the family home. Wasn't that what all aristocrats inevitably did? Shouldn't he be accustomed to the cold, from having crawled around on the icy flagstones as a chubby-cheeked toddler?

"Where were you before?" she asked.

Gilbert quirked an eyebrow.

"You'd be very surprised if I told you," he said, and that non-answer made her feel intensely curious. Where had he grown up? It was almost as if he didn't want her to know – or that he was used to not talking about it.

Everyone at Middlefield House seemed to have secrets they were keeping. And now, surprisingly, Gilbert himself had been added to that list.

"How long are you staying here?" she asked, seeing that he really did feel uneasy with the direction the conversation was taking.

"That depends on whether I can talk to Colin today or tomorrow," he admitted. "It's more likely to be tomorrow, because of all these birthday arrangements and the other guests arriving, and in that case, I'll be here until the day after." He sighed. "I think Colin will be a challenge. He seems like a rather argumentative person."

"That's how I read him as well," she said. "I think he's one of those who opposes an idea for the sake of it, and then needs to be talked around to it."

"That's very perceptive and could help me a lot," he said, sounding grateful. "Actually, what I should do then, is tell him he doesn't need any seeds, and let him convince me he does."

Mary laughed out loud at that, quickly clapping a hand over her mouth just like Sarah-Jane did, as she remembered somebody might hear her from outside the room.

"Is there anything I can bring you in the meantime?" she asked, remembering her place – and wanting to help him feel at home. "Tea? A gin and tonic? Cook made some very tasty-looking scones and Shrewsbury biscuits this morning."

The Shrewsbury biscuits, of which she'd sneaked one early in the morning, were delightful. Thin, crispy, baked to a perfect brown, with a hint of lemon zest, and dusted with sugar, they were the perfect accompaniment to a nice cup of tea. But Gilbert shook his head.

"I'm going to head out for a walk before the storm hits, if I can. I've been in the car most of the day and I'm longing to stretch my legs. Might already be too late, in which case I'll get wet," he said, with a rueful shrug.

She liked that he hadn't said he'd cancel his walk if it began to rain. Despite complaining about his freezing home, Gilbert clearly did enjoy walking in the rain. That was good because she did, too.

"I'd better be getting back to work," she said. "There's a lot to do, still. Lady Middlefield is definitely on the warpath in terms of getting things perfect."

As she turned, she saw that he was glancing at the back of her neck in a rather uncertain way. It took her just a moment to figure out what the problem was.

"Oh, dear. Is my hair still showing?"

"There's a very cheeky curl peeking out," he said.

She raised her hand and poked it blindly with her fingers, hoping that she'd managed to tuck the errant lock out of sight at last. But then, Gilbert said, "Wait a minute, Mary. Let me."

Standing still, feeling very surprised that he'd asked such a thing, she knew she was blushing all over again as he lifted the edge of her lacy cap.

Then, she felt his fingers stroking and smoothing her hair as he pushed it up to the nape of her neck. It didn't feel in the least like it did when Hannah, or one of the footmen, helped her with her hair. This felt a lot more gentle, a lot more deliberate. And he was taking far longer over it than either Hannah or the footman did.

Nor did Mary want him to stop.

In the end, as if he'd tucked the same lock back into place a few times and now realized that he had to step away, he put the edge of her cap gently down.

"All fixed," he said.

"Thank you," she said.

"I'll – I'll call you later if I need any tea or gin," he stammered.

She turned and stared at him, seeing that, strangely, his face looked a little flushed, too.

"Well, I'll – I'll speak to you later," she said. She couldn't get the memory of his touch out of her mind. In fact, Mary felt as if she wanted to go far away, to a dark room, and simply sit there and remember how his fingers had felt, stroking over her hair, and the very faint smell of sandalwood that she'd picked up on his skin, and the sound of his breathing.

She hugged herself hard, and then shook herself violently.

"Enough of this, Mary Adams," she told herself sternly, as she marched down the passage that led to the billiards room, where she now needed to stoke the fire. "Enough of this. You have work to do and can't spend the entire day mooning over these memories!"

But as she entered the billiards room, with its large green baize table, and its polished cues in a rack against the wall, and its smart blue carpet – it felt as if Gilbert's memory had walked right in behind her.

Mary had to admit that she was well and truly smitten.

But was he? And could anything come of it?

She was so preoccupied with her thoughts that it took her a moment to realize that there was somebody in the billiards room, sitting in the large leather covered wingback chair.

In fact, *two* somebodies.

And their body language as they heard her footsteps, made all Mary's instincts start flaring.

CHAPTER FIVE

The first head to peek over the chair, with a shocked expression on his face, was none other than Colin Middlefield. The man that Gilbert had come here to do business with! The heir to the estate.

And then, a moment later, with a flurry of skirts, a woman quickly left the selfsame chair and rushed over to the tapestry on the wall, staring at the embroidered hunting scene as if fascinated by it.

To her surprise, Mary recognized this woman. She was the daughter of the lord who owned the neighboring estate. Lady Ainsley was her name. There had been a neighbor's dinner a week or two ago, and she'd been here then. Sitting next to her husband, just as Colin Middlefield had been sitting next to his wife.

And yet, something about that panicked haste with which they had moved as she'd approached, made Mary wonder if there was more between them.

"You know, you shouldn't just barge into a room like that," Colin admonished Mary, irritation audible in his voice. "Maids should always knock first. You might be new here, but you'd better learn the right etiquette, fast!"

"It's always difficult to re-educate maids who've learned bad habits." Preening her silvery blond hair, Lady Ainsley glanced around, looking down her slender, aquiline nose at Mary. "We always prefer to train ours from scratch, though I understand it sometimes can't be done."

"We were short-staffed. We needed help. People should know these things!" Colin said.

Mary sighed inwardly, while maintaining as calm a demeanor as possible in the face of this unfair criticism, that she had to admit was veering into the territory of bullying. If it hadn't been for the conversation with Gilbert that she'd so recently had, it would have been a lot harder to keep her composure.

But the memory of his words, of his touch, so warm and kind, fortified her, and she reminded herself that these two were just being childish.

They were, in fact, showing their own guilt in the way they were hitting out at her insultingly. Having been discovered – well, almost discovered – doing something they shouldn't have been getting up to at all, they were quickly seeking to transfer the blame to her. Unfair as it was, that was how it went.

They both left the room, looking miffed, before Mary had had a chance to reply at all. In any case, there hadn't been anything to say.

After all, if she'd tried to speak up in her own defense, they would have taken even more offense. It wasn't fair being a servant sometimes. Most of the time you were invisible, and on the occasions when you weren't, there was usually a negative reason for it.

She took a look at the logs, deciding that a few more would be needed if this cold snap really hit, especially with guests aplenty needing to be warmed.

Leaving the room to fetch the logs, she picked up two empty wineglasses as she left. So they'd been enjoying an intimate drink in here together… and then things had gotten very friendly, very fast.

She almost collided with Sarah-Jane as she reached the back corridor. Sarah-Jane was in the same situation she'd been in – half buried under a mound of belongings she was carrying.

"Dearie me!" she exclaimed. "What a day! I must say, although I've worked here a couple of years, doing all these different chores today has made it feel like I'm somewhere brand new. Such an odd feeling. Somehow, it's an entirely different manor house today."

"Do you need any help with anything?" Mary asked, taking in Sarah-Jane's stressed demeanor. She guessed she'd been in the wrong place at the wrong time, with so many people frantically rushing around and issuing orders to any servant they could find.

"I think I'm sorted for now," she said, taking the opportunity to fan her face with her hands. "I've just been making a bed up on the third floor at lightning speed. That Miss Janet Middlefield keeps her room very warm! She has a massive fire burning inside it all day, even though she's not there. I didn't even know."

Mary widened her eyes. "That's rather wasteful," she agreed. This might be a big stately home, but hadn't the war taught anybody about the value of making do, and being thrifty when you could?

Janet was the younger of the grandchildren, a slight young woman in her teens, with a naturally frowning face and a preoccupied air. She had a love for piano and could often be found practicing her music in the parlor. Now that Mary thought of it, that room was also kept very warm.

She thought personally that Janet's enthusiasm for piano surpassed her talent by a considerable distance, but it wasn't in her to be critical of anybody who was following their passion. After all, striving to make music was a worthy pursuit. And if Janet got it right one day, then the parlor would be filled with beautiful harmonies.

Sarah-Jane continued. "After that, I had to take a whole pile of extra horse blankets to the stables, as they're going to need them tonight. And then, I was over in the west wing, cleaning a whole lot of rooms that are usually somebody else's duty entirely. Did you know that we have three different cellars in this manor house?"

"Three?" Mary echoed, surprised. "I thought we just had one, that really large cellar with all the wine racks, and that card table where Colin Middlefield sometimes has card games with his friends?"

"No. There are another two in the other wing. And spooky places they are, I can tell you!" Sarah-Jane shivered theatrically. "I'm glad that job's done. And before I do anything more, I'm off to get some lunch. Mind you also remember to eat, will you, dear? No point in working yourself to the bone and forgetting about your meals. Especially with this big dinner on tonight, that'll see all of us working late."

"I'll remember to eat," Mary promised, grateful for Sarah-Jane's kindness. She was such a thoughtful woman, and had taken Mary and Hannah under her wing since they had arrived.

Mary was excited about the dinner, because it would mean being in and out of the dining room doing the clearing away, and possibly even the serving. That would bring her into proximity with Gilbert again. She hoped that if she served him, she'd do it perfectly, and that her shyness around him wouldn't make her spill anything.

With another quick smile, Sarah Jane went on her way, and at that moment, footsteps from the other direction told Mary that this time, she'd been caught in the wrong place at the wrong time.

"You, there!" Mrs. Inglethorpe's voice was high and authoritative. "I need you, Mary! We have a serious situation you will have to help with. There has been – what I can only call – a terrible disaster!"

CHAPTER SIX

"What has happened?" Mary asked. Never, in her month of employment so far, had she seen Mrs. Inglethorpe look so distressed.

"Lady Mersey's cat has escaped from its room," Mrs. Inglethorpe announced.

"Oh, no! Snowdon? I brought him in!" Mary asked, feeling horrified. She'd only just taken the cat into that room – well, that was what it had felt like. She was shocked to discover that it was already late afternoon and several hours of intense work had passed since then.

"You know the animal's name, and have seen him? That's good," Mrs. Inglethorpe said. "Lady Mersey just returned to her room to dress for dinner, and discovered him missing. Apparently the window was open and she believes the feline could have pushed his way through, and escaped. He is, apparently, a very intelligent cat."

"Out in this weather?" Mary said, horrified. Rain was pummeling the windows. The winter storm had well and truly set in. "That's dreadful!"

"Yes. Out in this weather. The lady is most distressed and has asked us to search for him immediately. Since you are familiar with the cat, I would like you to take on this very important job. I don't care how long it takes – Lady Mersey wants that cat found and returned to the Green Room, preferably before dinner is finished and the birthday cake is cut."

"I'll do so straight away," Mary said.

"There are raincoats hung on the hook by the front door, and you'll find an umbrella there, too," Mrs. Inglethorpe said. The sound of her pen on her clipboard made a loud, scratching sound before she turned away.

Filled with anxiety over Snowdon's predicament, Mary hurried straight to the front door, moving aside to hug the wall as Colin, dressed in an evening jacket and now accompanied by his wife in a glittering green gown, headed for the drawing room. From there, the sounds of a piano – played well, by somebody other than Janet Middlefield, could be heard, the keys softly chiming.

The standard lamp in the corner was turned on, its red shade providing a warm ambiance, and the clink of crystal told Mary that guests were partaking of the array of drinks on offer, helped out by the head butler and his assistant.

Up until five minutes ago, she would have thought she'd have been heading to the kitchen, where she recalled roast duck breast and potatoes Dauphinoise, with their unctuous creaminess, being on the menu along with a selection of roasted vegetables.

The guests were going to eat like kings and queens tonight, and until recently, Mary had imagined she'd be in a fresh apron and cap, part of the kitchen service.

Now, another and more important task awaited her – finding a missing pet.

Walking quickly past the parlor door, she headed to the coat stand in the hall, and put on a raincoat and a waterproof hat, taking an umbrella from the rack.

The poor cat! Out in this weather! Snowdon must be seriously annoyed with his own life decisions, she thought, opening the big front door, which nearly slammed in her face and knocked her off her feet as a gust of wind grabbed it.

Trying again, this time, Mary successfully managed to get through the door. It was blowing a gale outside. The wind was accompanied by rain so cold and brutal that at times it was turning to stinging sleet. She gasped for breath as a rogue gust of wet, freezing wind found its way unerringly under the collar of her raincoat and trickled down her spine, its icy progress causing her to shiver. Her hair was already sopping wet, the hat having been blown off as soon as she exited the door. Perhaps it was lodged in the same hedge where the chauffeur's top hat had been, she wondered.

At any rate, armed only with a leaky raincoat, and an umbrella that was threatening to turn inside out at any moment, Mary headed around the manor house, her shoes squelching as she walked.

One thing was for sure, no cat would be out in the open in this weather. Snowdon, having escaped from the window, would soon have realized the folly of his decision and would be looking for somewhere to shelter.

Now, that room was in the west wing on the second floor. A thick creeper as well as a drainpipe would have provided the footholds needed for a cat to climb down. But then, where would Snowdon have gone?

Battling the gusting wind, Mary fought her way around to that side of the manor house. Standing on the paved walkway that surrounded the large, imposing stone building, she stared up.

Lady Mersey's bedroom was the second one in the row. That meant the second window? But there seemed to be an additional window there, one that was darkened, in between the two brightly lit rooms, one with ivory curtains, and one with blue – Gilbert's room. How strange. Clearly, this manor house must have additional rooms or passages that she didn't know about. At any rate, now she'd identified the ivory curtains, and had seen the path down the creeper that Snowdon must have taken.

Now, where was the closest place to shelter?

Could the cat have climbed back in through another window? That was her first idea, but looking at the manor house's frontage, she saw that all the windows were firmly closed. So none of them would have been a possible route in.

Now, if Snowdon had gotten this far down and landed with those fluffy paws of his on this selfsame walkway, then where would he have headed?

To the right, the walkway led to the edge of the house, beyond which Mary saw a small summerhouse – now disused, but probably a beautiful place in the sunny season for people to sit with a cup of tea or a gin and tonic. At least that provided some shelter, so maybe he'd headed straight there?

"Snowdon!" she called as she walked, knowing that the spattering of the rain was far louder than her own voice. Her shoes were already squelching horribly in the damp. "Snowdon, where are you? Pss pss pss!"

She reached the summer house and peered inside. It was very cold and drafty and there was no sign at all of any cat. She didn't think a cat would have chosen to shelter here. The cover was too flimsy, and rain was gusting under the octagonal roof.

Was there anywhere beyond? She could see a light in the distance that indicated the stables. Well, it was far away, but at least that was a solid shelter, and a clever cat could have decided to make a frantic dash for it.

Going much more slowly than she imagined Snowdon would have done, Mary slipped and slid her way down the wet grass, with rain now sluicing over it. She was shivering from the cold. A raincoat was insufficient for this storm. A massive great overcoat would have been better.

She reached the stables and headed inside, breathing in the smell of straw and horse, and feeling a gust of warmth go some way toward thawing her freezing face.

"Well, you look like a drowned rat!"

The voice surprised her, and she spun around. There, on the other side of the main door, was an elderly groom, with gray hair, who had a flask of tea in his hand and was sitting on a straw bale.

"Hello," Mary said through chattering teeth. "I'm Mary Adams, one of the housemaids."

He extended a gnarled hand. Mary shook it, with fingers that she couldn't properly feel.

"And I'm Dickens, the head groom here. I ain't seen you before?" he asked.

"I'm new. I've been here a month," she said.

"Ah. I just got back from me holidays with my son, down in Leicester," he said. "That would account for why I haven't seen you around. But what are you doing here now?"

"I'm looking for a cat. One of the guests brought a cat along, and he's gone missing."

Dickens frowned. "Well, I've definitely seen no cat. We have a couple of stable cats down 'ere, and if any intruder set foot in this barn, they'd raise the alarm with their yowling and hissing. So you can be confident he's not 'ere. But have some tea, while you are."

Turning back to his flask, he filled the cup and handed it to her, and Mary took a big gulp of the hot, sweet tea.

"Why are you here so late?" she asked.

"I'm stayin' up to watch one of the horses. There was huntin' earlier today, before the weather turned, and Conker here, the chestnut, gets well excited after his hunts. Takes 'im a long time to settle, remembering what fun he had gallopin' around the countryside. I came to check him and to make sure he hadn't broken out in a sweat again."

Mary peeked into the stall. The large, chestnut horse looked calm to her, munching at a big pile of hay with a satisfied expression on its enormous face, while cozily tucked up in a brown and white striped blanket, and Dickens' approving nod showed that he agreed with her highly uneducated opinion.

She finished the tea, feeling slightly less freezing.

“You carryin’ on with this search?” Dickens asked in a concerned way.

“Yes, I have to,” Mary said. “You know, I feel so anxious for this poor cat. Imagine being out in this weather. Snowdon must be feeling so confused and scared.”

“Humph,” the head groom said, pouring himself some tea. “I’ve never known a stupid cat. And my opinion is, if this cat’s as clever as most, he won’t have gone far. Maybe he hasn’t even left the premises.” He gave her a knowing look.

“What do you mean by that?” Mary asked, intrigued.

“Oh, I mean that you should search much closer to home.” The head groom leaned closer, dropping his voice to a conspiratorial whisper. “Remember, this manor house was built in the days when people wanted to protect their valuables from the marauding northerners. Let that be your guide.”

CHAPTER SEVEN

"What do you mean by that?" Her curiosity thoroughly aroused, Mary leaned closer, but Dickens shut his mouth firmly and stood back, regarding the horse with a contented expression on his own face as he sipped his tea.

He was going to say no more, that was clear.

Mary left the stable yard feeling thoroughly intrigued. It was a wrench to venture back into the cold, which had if anything gotten worse, but at least she now had some hot tea inside her, and also, she was motivated by Dickens' words.

Close to home?

Thinking about that phrase, and also about Snowdon's obvious intelligence, Mary was coming to a different conclusion. And that was that Snowdon had never gone out of the window at all. It had already been a breezy, rainy afternoon, and he hadn't seemed like a cat who would have wanted to get his paws wet.

So maybe he'd found some kind of hiding place within the room itself?

That was Mary's new theory, as she headed back to the manor house, now hurrying through the rain, pausing only to retrieve her hat from where it had been lodged in the hedge.

She headed in the front door, realizing that she was dripping everywhere as she went into the cloakroom on the far side of the hall. She was soaked to the bone, and her hair was plastered to her head in wet rat's tails. Her cap was now so wet she could squeeze water out of it.

Quickly, she folded the umbrella and placed it back on the stand, where it instantly began to drip. Then she peeled off the raincoat and hung that up, too. And then, she took off her shoes. They were so wet that they were going to leave great big puddles every time she moved. She'd have to go barefoot for now and get back to her room to put on a fresh pair at the first opportunity.

For now, though, it was time to find out if Dickens had been correct. If not, she'd have to go back out into the rain again. Mary fervently hoped, for the sakes of both herself and the cat, that his theory was correct and that Snowdon had been hiding closer to home.

Even in her bare feet, the hem of her dress was still drenched, splattering against her ankles every time she took a step. Dripping gently, she tiptoed past the drawing room, seeing to her relief that everyone had left that room, and gone through to the main dining room for dinner. The most delicious smells were emanating from there, making her remember that the two thick slices of fruit and nut bread she'd devoured had been a long time ago.

But it was Snowdon she needed to worry about now. Missing his dinner would be – as Lady Middlefield liked to say – a catastrophe. With the emphasis, this time, on 'cat'.

Mary headed upstairs, her soles numb and her toes stinging from the cold. Reaching Lady Mersey's room, she tapped on the door.

Entering, she closed it very quickly behind her. If for any reason, Snowdon was in the room and feeling restless once more, she didn't want him nipping out of the door. Once she was certain that wouldn't happen, she turned back and surveyed the room.

There was a fire flickering in the grate, and the room was toasty warm. In fact, Mary could feel the hem of her gown start to steam gently as she stood there, feeling a little like a trespasser in this private space, because she wasn't bringing anything or fetching anything, but rather, searching for something.

Now, where could an adventurous cat, freed from the confines of his cage and wanting to stretch his legs, have gone that wasn't outside?

In one of the cupboards?

Feeling even more like an intruder now, Mary moved to the closer of the two wardrobes, and opened it.

The wardrobe was filled with fur coats and tweed skirts and waxed jackets, clearly the wardrobe that the lady was using for the really bad weather clothing. There was no cat inside. Mary made very sure, searching carefully and calling all the while. She'd personally thought that the furs might be a good nesting place, but Snowdon had thought differently.

What about the other one? The door was ajar because of a bulky garment inside. Maybe the gap was big enough to allow a cat to slip in?

Mary pushed the garments aside – this was the cupboard for the ball gowns and shoes. As she worked, she moved each dress carefully aside, checking the back of the cupboard. It was protected by big wooden boards – lighter at the edges, but much darker toward the middle of the wardrobe.

Why would it be so much darker?

Putting her hand out into the darkness, she found to her shock that the boards didn't exist at all. There was a sizeable gap in them, about two feet wide by three feet high.

Mary caught her breath as she felt around the boards, with chilly air emanating from the space beyond. What Dickens had said was absolutely correct. There were tunnels bac,k routes, and secret compartments in this manor house. She'd just found one. Easily enough space for a cat to go through – a person could even squeeze in there, although she had no idea what lay beyond.

Mary leaned inside the cupboard, glimpsing a stone-lined tunnel stretching into the darkness beyond the gap, and called, "Psspsspss? Snowdon?"

From somewhere down the tunnel, she heard a faint meow. Then, the padding of paws was audible. And finally, a furry face, with a smudge of dust across the spotless white coat, appeared in the gap.

"Oh, Snowdon! You had us all so worried!"

Mary gathered the cat up in her arms, feeling his warm, furry weight nestle into her as he started purring. She raised a finger and rubbed his whiskers, and he writhed his head against her hand, in evident ecstasy.

Backing away from the wardrobe, not caring how wet and dirty she was, but filled with a sense of immense relief, she deposited the cat on the bed. He began kneading the spotless ivory bedcover, looking pleased to be back in the civilized world after his adventure.

Now, although the spoiled pet was at liberty to enjoy the freedom of the Green Room, how was she going to stop him getting back in that passage? She wasn't sure if the china bowl on the floor, containing the choicest pieces of cooked chicken, or the saucer of water, or the spacious sand tray in the corner, filled with fragrant soil for him to do his business, or even the fun of kneading the bedcovers, would be enough to curb this cat's strong sense of adventure.

Was there a way of closing up this gap?

Pushing the ball gowns aside, Mary crawled all the way into the wardrobe. On the side of the gap, she discovered a section of planks that felt movable. When she tugged at it, it moved across smoothly, as if on hidden rollers, covering the gap like a sliding door. There was even a latch, with a small clasp on it, on the side of the wooden piece.

And she found a brass catch on the back of the wardrobe that it fitted into. Once it had clicked into place, she didn't think that an adventurous cat could possibly nudge it away.

A wardrobe with a false back, that led into a narrow passage, which led who knew where? What other strange secrets did this manor house contain, she wondered. At any rate, it was time to go back downstairs, find the head housekeeper, and deliver the news that the missing cat was found.

Mary hurried out, closing the door carefully behind her, and hustled back to the first floor, where the sumptuous aromas of caramel and chocolate told her that dessert was already underway.

"I found him," she told Mrs. Inglethorpe, who was standing in the kitchen together with the cook, and Howard the assistant to Lady Middlefield. All three of them were supervising the plating of the dessert.

Clipboard in hand, the housekeeper turned, looking surprised and pleased.

"Good work, Mary! I'll tell her as soon as we take these plates through," she said, her tone making Mary feel hopeful about that shared day off with Hannah. This was sounding as if it was promising. Deciding that she had better let the housekeeper know about this strange exit point in the Ivory Room, she continued.

"He'd gone through an opening at the back of the wardrobe. I closed it up again."

"Leftovers from when they renovated the plumbing, I'm sure," Mrs. Inglethorpe said dismissively, seemingly not that concerned about the secret passage Mary had found.

"Now, that piece of cake is not at the right angle compared to the others, and it's substantially smaller," Howard said fussily, and everyone's attention was back on the pudding again.

Since she was in no state to go through to the dining room to be seen by the guests, Mary remained in the kitchen, helping to ferry the dishes from the countertop to the scullery. Luckily, the kitchen was warm, and after a busy half-hour of cleaning and tidying, she'd steamed herself mostly dry and was feeling warm again.

The dining room was quiet, and faintly, the sounds of piano music could be heard again, this time, coming from the parlor.

And finally, the birthday dinner was over, and with the kitchen tidied, that meant they could all gather in the staff pantry, and enjoy some of the birthday leftovers.

There was enough of the roast duck left for everyone to have a portion and roast vegetables in abundance. There were even some of the potatoes Dauphinoise, which Mary thought were frankly delicious. It seemed impossible that the humble potato, which had never struck her as good for much except roasting and mashing, could be so transformed by thin slicing, the addition of butter and cream, and a lengthy baking time.

She and Hannah rolled their eyes blissfully each other as they cleaned their plates, standing with their backs against the wall because the staff pantry was so crowded. In the throngs, Mary glanced around for Sarah-Jane, hoping to see her there and find out how she had enjoyed the duck, but she was nowhere in sight.

Perhaps they still needed one or two of the housemaids on duty in the parlor. Mary hoped there would be some duck left over for her later.

For now, though, it was time to head to bed. From outside, Mary could hear the sound of cars, their tires scrunching over the gravel as those guests who lived nearby, made their departure.

What a day it had been! She hoped, now that these festivities were over, things would get back to the way they'd been when she'd arrived at Middlefield Manor. Everything had been much calmer then.

As she quickly flitted from the service corridor, to the staircase that would take her up to her bedroom, voices rang out from behind her and she quickly turned, her heart speeding up as she recognized Gilbert's tone. Quickly, she tweaked at the hem of her dress, which was still damp, and rather dirty too, thanks to her outdoor adventures.

Gilbert was talking to Colin, and to Lady Ainsley, the pretty neighbor that Mary had seen Colin with earlier in the billiards room. Both of them seemed to be in a good mood now and were smiling and laughing as they said their goodbyes.

But, as he saw Mary, Gilbert looked directly at her and mouthed, "Good night," giving her a quick grin.

"Good night!" Mary mouthed right back at him.

Feeling cheered by that brief interaction, she headed up to bed. At least there were no more chores to do today, she thought, taking off her uniform at last and placing it in the laundry bag, and then brushing out her hair, which was full of knots and tangles from her time out in the rain.

Her bedroom was small, but from the narrow window, she had a view of the fields behind the estate and the edge of the stable block. At this hour, everything was dark, although she caught the sweeping shadows that fell over the grass as some of the last guests departed.

"Well, what a day," Mary said to herself. "At least that's it now, and I can get some rest!"

But it seemed like only a moment after she'd closed her eyes that the insistent sound of the buzzer jerked her awake again, its sound unexpected, and briefly scary.

The buzzer, directly to her small room. Summoning her?

She sat bolt upright, her dreams dissolving, staring into the darkness as she fumbled for her lamp.

Who could want a housemaid, now in what felt like the middle of the night?

CHAPTER EIGHT

The yellowish lamplight bathed Mary's small room in its glow as she looked at the system of switches and pulleys on her room's wall. There were four possibilities – Lady Middlefield's suite, the parlor, the drawing-room, and the kitchen.

Her first thought was that Lady Middlefield had a crisis and had perhaps fallen in the night.

But it wasn't her pulley that was buzzing. It was the one for the kitchen.

Someone was there, summoning her, at a very silent, dark and late hour?

Mary shivered as she dressed with frantic haste. There was something very strange about this. Who would be there at such a time? And why her?

Had there been some catastrophe like a shelf collapsing, she wondered. Maybe a few people had been called, and it would be a case of all hands on deck. She quickly buttoned her navy blue blouse, slipped on her other pair of shoes – this one, thankfully dry – and headed downstairs.

It really was late. She'd never walked around alone at this hour in this manor house before, and had to admit that it felt eerie. The storm had cleared, and a shaft of moonlight was peeking from behind the clouds as she passed the grandfather clock. It was just before midnight, and her quick footsteps were the only sound, apart from some faint, faraway snoring.

She ducked into the service corridor and hurried to the scullery entrance, still uneasily aware that she seemed to be the only person responding to a buzzer, and that nobody else appeared to have been called.

Maybe she should be careful, Mary thought, with an instinctive shiver.

She walked into the kitchen quietly, feeling the hairs on the back of her neck stand up.

And then, with a bang and a clatter, something erupted from the servants' pantry. Mary spun around, letting out a sharp squeak of alarm as her heart jumped into her throat.

Wild-eyed and frantic, it was Sarah-Jane.

"Mary," she whispered. "I need – I need to tell you something. Something dreadful, that I've just found out about!"

Mary stared at her in consternation. By the faint overhead light, she saw that Sarah-Jane looked more distressed than she'd ever seen her. She had no idea that she could even look so upset. Her usually good-natured face was drawn into lines of tension. Her eyes were wild, and she was breathing fast.

"I've – I've just come in from – from…" she gabbled.

Mary's stomach clenched. She had no idea what could have happened or what was making Sarah-Jane so terribly distressed.

"It's alright," she soothed her, even though she was now in a state of tension also, just from seeing Sarah-Jane's behavior. "Take your time and calm down. Breathe."

That might not be the right thing to say, she corrected herself. Sarah-Jane was already breathing so hard she was practically panting.

"Breathe *slowly*," Mary further advised.

She grasped the other woman's hands, feeling that they were shaking. Well, this was all so strange and upsetting that Mary's hands were unsteady, too.

"I can't – I can't tell you now." Her voice dropped to a whisper and she stared around, as if there might be somebody peering in from the larder door, or the pantry entrance.

"Why not?" Mary whispered back. She was getting more and more alarmed by the sheer extent of Sarah-Jane's behavior and the distressing change in her demeanor. Whatever this was, it seemed extremely serious.

"Walls have ears!" Sarah-Jane said, her gaze darting from one wall to the other. The tone in which she spoke made shivers trickle all the way down Mary's spine.

"Well, you obviously do need to get this off your chest," Mary said, but at that moment, a thumping noise from somewhere outside made Sarah-Jane freeze.

"What's that?" she breathed, eyes wide.

"I – I don't know." Trying to control her own panic, Mary thought frantically of what it might be. "Maybe it was that loose piece of guttering near the kitchen? There's still a wind blowing."

But Sarah-Jane looked unconvinced.

"We need to get out of here," she muttered. "Meet me in – in the carriage house, in an hour's time. That's far from anywhere. There won't be anybody there. Then I'll tell you."

"Can't you tell me now, quietly?" Mary pleaded. This seemed like a very serious situation. She wanted to know exactly what was making this usually placid and friendly woman seem on the verge of a panicked meltdown.

"I can't," she hissed.

She was too afraid, Mary saw that. Not only had she become temporarily paranoid, genuinely believing that walls did in fact have ears, but she was also mostly incoherent.

"Do you want to come to my room and sit down for a while?" she offered, in the quietest whisper possible, but Sarah-Jane shook her head violently.

"I want to – I want to make sure the coast's clear," she whispered back. "You go to your room. And only come out when it's time for our meeting."

Now, Mary's stomach was churning. This was all so unprecedented. She had no idea what this could be about, and it was unsettling her as much as it seemed to be unsettling Sarah-Jane.

"Is this about somebody in particular?" she hazarded, getting up from her chair. Well, she had no choice about that, because Sarah-Jane had gotten up too, from her precarious perch on the edge of her wooden stool.

"It's somebody who – he is not what he seems. Be careful."

And then, without saying anything further, Sarah-Jane hurried out of the servants' pantry and disappeared down the corridor that led to her room.

"Wait!" Jumping to her feet, Mary hurried to the doorway. "Sarah-Jane! Come back, please!"

But she was gone.

Should she follow her?

Reluctantly, Mary decided she'd have to do what Sarah-Jane had asked, even if it meant an agonizing wait, and she somehow felt she was making the wrong choice.

Feeling extremely troubled, Mary hurried back to her own quarters. Walls have ears? People are not what they seem.

As she went back up the winding staircase to her room, walking quietly and finding herself much more alarmed by every small creak, groan, and faraway snore, Mary tried to puzzle out what the background to all of this might be.

"He is not what he seems." What had that even meant?

It seemed to her that Sarah-Jane must have stumbled across something – information, or a secret – that she'd learned very recently. That would explain the sudden change in her demeanor. With so many people all doing different tasks, perhaps Sarah-Jane had been exposed to something she hadn't known about before. That seemed the most likely explanation, Mary reasoned.

Perhaps she'd overreacted to it. But with a chill, she remembered the woman's usually calm temperament. She didn't seem like somebody who would overreact.

The sound of the grandfather clock striking a quarter past midnight made her jump as she passed.

At least, if she listened carefully from her room, she'd be able to hear the clock striking one, and then it would be time to head out to the carriage house.

Mary's mouth felt dry. How she wished she knew more about the situation.

There was no way she could even lie down. She perched on the edge of her bed, listening out for the grandfather clock's chime, and playing and replaying this strange conversation in her head over and over.

What should she ask Sarah-Jane, when she saw her again? What if she was still reluctant to talk about it? Briefly, Mary wondered if she should bring Hannah along, but decided against it. One sleepless, worried and disturbed person was enough. Hannah had also had a tiring day - and Mary was the person that Sarah-Jane had chosen to confide in. She, and she alone, would have to learn the truth here.

At this late hour, the wind was blowing strongly, howling through the tiny gap in the window so that she had to keep her door open in case she missed the chiming of the clock. A couple of times, she went down to the landing to check the clock, just in case.

Finally, the clock struck the hour. She heard the single chime very faintly and sprang to her feet.

At last, she could find out what this was all about. What a stressful hour it had been.

But she'd need to be careful. The worry and the distress in Sarah-Jane's voice had been very real.

Whatever this was, secrecy and caution were definitely advised.

Once again, feeling even more unsure than she had the first time she'd left her room that night, Mary crept downstairs, looking left and right carefully, listening out for any sight or sound.

Was that footsteps, receding rapidly in the distance? Or was it just the wind rattling that loose window frame in the corridor? For a moment, it was impossible to tell, and her hands felt cold. But there was no further sound, so she decided it must have been a rogue gust of wind.

She tiptoed along the corridor, heading for the scullery door. This was always left unlocked at night so that the household staff could come and go as needed. Although most of the maids slept in, there were a few who lived in the nearby village.

The scullery door was open, and the doormat was damp. So people had been in and out recently.

She stepped outside, shivering in the icy wind. A paved pathway led to the carriage house. It was well used, and easy to follow, even in the cloudy darkness.

Wondering if she was going to regret her actions -but unable to let her friend down – she crept along the path.

There was the carriage house ahead, a large, stone building that contained several carriages, harnesses, as well as two of the vehicles that were used on the estate and a newer workhorse – a Ford tractor.

There was a clanging noise coming from inside. Hearing it, Mary hesitated.

"Sarah-Jane?" she called softly. Goosebumps were cascading down her spine, and not just from the cold. If Sarah-Jane had not personally asked her to come out here, while in a distressed state, Mary knew she would have turned back.

But instead, she pushed open the door and stepped inside.

"Sarah-Jane?"

The carriage house seemed deserted. The shapes of the carriages and the tractor were visible, darker outlines in the gloom. There was nothing else to be seen, apart from a discarded pile of dark sacking in the corner.

Dark sacking?

Suddenly rethinking that idea, feeling a terrible coldness, Mary remembered that the carriage house, like every other part of Middlefield Manor, had been thoroughly cleaned and tidied in preparation for the grand dame's birthday. There would be no piles of sacking lying around.

In any case, as her legs took her closer, seemingly of their own volition, she discovered that the nearer she got, the less this looked like sacking.

Now, she could see the shape of an arm. And now, the white blur of a face.

And then, in horror, Mary was looking down at the wide-eyed, unseeing form of her friend, Sarah Jane.

She was lying still. She was not breathing.

And the deep gash in her forehead told Mary, without a doubt, that she had been murdered.

CHAPTER NINE

Mary didn't remember much about the next few minutes. Somehow, she ended up back in Middlefield Manor, in the kitchen. Somebody was screaming. That somebody was her. She had her back against the wall, and people were running toward her, running to find out what had happened. The cook, the butler, Mrs. Inglethorpe herself. All the servants were first to arrive, thanks to their proximity to the kitchen.

"The carriage house!" That was her voice, high and shrill. "Sarah-Jane is there, and she's been murdered! The carriage house!"

She was shaking all over. Lights were snapped on. Someone – she couldn't remember who – led her over to the kitchen table and sat her down. She heard voices and running footsteps over the blasting of the wind, and then – from the direction of the carriage house – a volley of shocked cries.

Someone made her a cup of tea. She didn't even register it happening until she blinked and saw it steaming in front of her. Then, the next moment, Hannah was there.

"Mary!"

Her friend raced across the kitchen, looking red-eyed and mussy-haired after having been roused from an exhausted sleep. "Mary, what's happened?"

Hannah grabbed Mary's cold hands in both of her own warm ones.

"It – it's Sarah-Jane," Mary stammered out. "She's dead. Someone killed her!"

Hannah gasped. Her face froze in shock, and then, a moment later, tears flooded her eyes.

"Sarah-Jane? Is that – is that why everyone's running to the carriage house?" she asked softly.

Mary nodded. "She's there. And there's more to it."

She didn't dare say another word, though, because there were other people around, and she had no idea who might have done this, or why.

Sarah-Jane was dead! Her cheerful, funny, kind friend. Never again would she see her smiling face, or meet up with her in the staff pantry for a cuppa, or walk into a bedroom and find her changing a pillowcase with her trademark enthusiasm.

Dead.

It was bleak and final, and Mary found herself dissolving into tears of grief as Hannah held her hand tightly.

As if in a dream, she watched people come and go. To her astonishment, as she wiped away yet another flood of tears, she saw Lady Middlefield herself, wrapped in a fur coat and with a scarf over her hair, heading through the kitchen toward the scullery door, with her son Colin walking behind.

The wing where the Middlefields stayed was closest to the kitchens, so maybe they'd overheard the commotion, or somebody had gone and woken them up.

"Mother, I don't think you should go to the carriage house," Colin was saying, his voice as nervous and unsure as she'd ever heard it.

"Don't tell me what to do! This has happened on my property and I intend to take a look," Lady Middlefield said in imperious tones as she strode out of the kitchen door.

Mary bowed her head again.

Her friend had been so scared. She had found something out – and it had gotten her killed.

This felt so terrible, so final, that for the next few minutes, Mary felt mired in misery, and believed that this was a low point in her life that could not possibly get any worse.

But then, as she started to think more rationally, and her brain began to move past the paralyzing sense of sadness, Mary realized things *could* get worse.

And they were going to.

She had no idea who could have killed Sarah-Jane.

There was nobody else who could have committed this crime that she knew of. Nobody had been around in the manor house. She hadn't seen a soul. What did that mean?

Mary felt sick as she realized the inevitable conclusion.

As the first person on the scene, she was going to be a suspect. They would believe that she'd committed this murder, by the fact that she'd been there at the time, and nobody else had been around.

This horrific situation had just become a thousand times worse. It felt like a repeat of the tragedy, and the aftermath, that had played out at Coldstream Lodge.

Burying her head in her hands, for a few long, desolate minutes, all Mary could do was to hide away from a world that seemed colder and crueler than she'd ever believed it could be.

She only raised her head when Hannah let go her hands abruptly. The hasty scrape of a chair followed, and a voice said, from the kitchen door, "So, is this the witness?"

Looking up, Mary saw that the police had arrived.

A suave-looking policeman, with graying hair and a sleek mustache, was staring at her with his arms folded. Behind him, Colin was hovering attentively.

"Yes, Inspector Braham," he said, in tones politer than Mary had ever heard him use. "This is the kitchen maid who found the deceased. Her name is, er…"

Clearly, he had no idea of Mary's name, and she was temporarily too hoarse to reply, but Hannah leaped to her feet, and to the rescue.

"This is Mary Adams, sir," she said, standing bravely in front of her friend.

"I see." The inspector moved a few steps sideways. He regarded her through narrowed eyes, and Mary stared back at him. She didn't see any clemency in his piercing gaze.

Her stomach twisted.

"I'll speak to you alone, miss," he said.

That was her cue to get up, she knew. Scrambling clumsily to her feet, she reached for Hannah's hand and gave it one last squeeze, before following the inspector. With every step she took, her stomach knotted tighter. This was a predicament where she was entirely powerless. It was a terrible feeling to be like this, at the mercy of the law.

Inspector Braham led her to the staff pantry, where Mary guessed that he might have been busy already, because the table was totally clear, apart from a notepad that was positioned squarely in the center.

The inspector sat down and opened the notepad. Mary sat opposite. Her tears had dried now, thanks to the icy flood of shock as she'd come to terms with her circumstances. And apprehension curdled inside her.

"Tell me what happened tonight, Miss Adams," the inspector said.

Mary took a deep breath. "Well, I was – I was woken in the night by the buzzer. It came from the kitchens, so I hurried down, and Sarah-Jane was there. She seemed very upset."

For a moment, the only sound was the deliberate scratching noise of the inspector's pen.

"And did she say why she was so upset?" he asked.

“Well, she said – she said she wanted to talk about it later, and didn’t want to say anything right here, on the premises, with other people around. That was why she asked me to meet her in the carriage house,” Mary said. She hoped that the inspector would understand, from her words, that Sarah-Jane hadn’t been upset with her, but had rather wanted to confide in her.

With a sense of inevitability, she realized that he would now ask if they had fought, if there had been any disagreement between them. But to her surprise, it seemed that Inspector Braham had not yet finished with his earlier questions.

“So she said nothing at all about why she was upset?”

Mary shook her head. "I – I know she'd been doing a lot of different jobs recently," she said. "We all had, thanks to the birthday party and sprucing up the place."

She was going to use this as a lead-in, to explain that Sarah-Jane could have found something out that she hadn’t known before.

But the inspector nodded as if Mary had given him a valuable tidbit of information.

“Upset because of having to do new jobs outside her normal scope of work,” he said thoughtfully.

That wasn’t right! Mary waited for him to ask her some more, so she could explain better.

But he didn’t. Instead, he went off on a surprising tangent.

“Working long hours, too, I suppose?”

“Yes, we all were,” Mary said, glad that he’d picked that up. That was why Sarah-Jane hadn’t had a chance to speak to her about this problem earlier. It was because she’d simply been too busy.

More scratching of the pen.

“So, this meant that you arranged to meet at one a.m.?”

“Yes, that’s correct.”

He hadn’t given her the opportunity to say what Sarah-Jane had told her, which was those strange words, “He’s not what he seems.”

It was going to be important, though, because in due course, the inspector was going to accuse her of having committed this crime. Then, those words could be her lifeline and could hopefully point him in the right direction to find the real killer.

“When you reached the meeting point, tell me what happened?”

“I – I went in. I didn’t see anyone there on the way, although I think I might have heard footsteps. But I wasn’t sure,” Mary admitted.

“And you entered the carriage house?”

"I did. It was – it was so dark. I didn't see her there at first, and then – then I saw her slumped in the corner. I could see – the terrible gash on her forehead."

What had made that? A steel bar? Some sort of heavy implement. It was too terrible to imagine the scenario, and Mary's mind recoiled from it.

"So it was very dark?"

"Yes, it was."

Why was he asking that? Was it a question he was going to use to try to prove her guilt? She swallowed nervously. So far all he'd done was set the scene, but she knew that the moment was drawing closer when he was going to pronounce her an official suspect, or maybe accuse her directly.

"Sarah-Jane and I were good friends," she said. "She was friendly to everyone, and I don't know anyone who would have wanted to kill her. Including myself, obviously."

How terrible to even have to say such a thing, but she knew that Sarah-Jane would have wanted her to clear her name.

"Absolutely."

The inspector wrote a few more lines in his notebook, stared down at the neat lettering, turned back a page to check something else, and then gave a decisive nod.

"I see. Thank you for your version, Miss Adams." His eyes regarded her, and she thought his gaze was surprisingly cold, for eyes that were such a rich color of blue.

"I – what else do you need?" This apprehension felt like too much. She wanted to get it over with. He must accuse her so that she didn't have to carry on dreading the moment when he would.

But the inspector closed his notebook.

"This must have been a very upsetting experience for you, Miss Adams," he said. "I trust that you will manage to overcome your grief and continue with your duties tomorrow?"

"I – I will." She blinked in shock. He wasn't only not accusing her, but he was also implying she could go about her work as normal. How was this possible?

It came to her in a blaze of insight.

Of course! This inspector must already have solved the crime, at record speed, while she was still sitting at the table and recovering from the shock. Maybe he'd had an early lead or else found a piece of evidence at the scene that hadn't been visible in the darkness.

That was obviously what had happened, and so all this time she'd been stewing in her fear and waiting to be taken into the police station, he had merely been wrapping up the loose ends of the case by asking a few routine questions.

But now, would she be brave enough to ask him a question?

For Sarah-Jane's sake, she would. She wanted to know who had committed this foul deed, and also why.

"Inspector?" she asked in a wobbly voice that was almost drowned out by the sound of his chair scraping back.

He stared at her with a hint of impatience. "Yes, Miss Adams?"

"May I ask – who did this? Are you making an arrest, or have you already made one?"

To her astonishment, Inspector Braham gave a fatherly chuckle.

"You clearly enjoy reading mystery novels, Miss Adams. Or else you have a fertile imagination."

"How do you mean?" she asked.

"It was very evident to me, after just a few moments at the scene, that this was an accidental death. Your co-worker, in the darkness and in a place strange to her, walked into something solid, which injured her so badly that death ensued. It's a real pity that she had been working so hard and felt overstressed. Possibly, as a more mature woman, she wasn't capable of meeting the demands which a younger maid like yourself would have easily managed. Clearly, that is why she was upset and didn't want to speak about it in her workplace itself."

Mary goggled at him in sheer amazement as he moved to the door.

"It's a tragic case of death by misadventure, and nobody is to blame except herself. Thank you for your cooperation in this matter."

He turned and left, leaving Mary at a loss for words.

The inspector was wrong. He must be. Because Mary knew she hadn't been wrong.

She'd seen how upset Sarah-Jane had been. Her friend had been frantic and terrified, and she'd uttered those words that Mary hadn't had a chance to tell the inspector, "He is not what he seems."

And what could she possibly have walked into when she'd been slumped next to a wall? There had been machinery there, but it had been a few yards away.

There was no doubt in Mary's mind that this was murder.

So, why was the inspector covering it up?

CHAPTER TEN

By the time Mary stumbled out of the staff pantry, still in a state of shock, the kitchen was quiet. With the inspector having left, everyone had gone to bed, and Mary decided there was no option but to do the same. Her head was spinning with confusion. This was all wrong.

She had been spared, and avoided the accusation she'd thought was a certainty. But nothing – nothing – felt right about it.

Maybe the morning would bring some insight. She urgently needed that.

As Mary headed down the quiet corridor, her state of shock began to change into something different.

And that was anger.

There was only one reason why this death could have been ruled accidental, and that was because the Middlefield family wanted it that way. They didn't want their name smeared, they didn't want the troubling accusations that a murder would bring.

She knew about that because she'd seen it before. Mary had been caught up in it before. What a way to learn how things worked. But she had learned.

Treading thoughtfully along the corridor's shiny flagstones, she realized that, of course, the Middlefields would not have wanted any trouble, especially on such an important occasion.

Somebody – one of the family – must have discussed this with the inspector. Maybe he'd agreed to keep the peace with these influential aristocrats, or maybe they'd even paid him to think that way.

It was a possibility that got Mary's temper flaring. She hadn't liked the expression in that inspector's eyes. There had been that strange coldness there. Maybe it was the type of coldness that appeared in somebody's eyes when they had decided to ignore the facts and go along with what they were told to do, while thinking about a lot of folded twenty-pound notes.

At that moment, she was jerked out of that unpleasant reverie, because she realized that the passage ahead of her wasn't empty. There was somebody standing there.

With a gasp, she focused. Dangerous things had happened tonight already, and even though the police denied it, she knew there was a killer on the loose.

But the person standing in front of her, wearing a green dressing gown and a worried expression, was Gilbert.

"Mary Adams," he said softly.

"Mr. MacLeod." Her voice wobbled. What a night it had been. Now, here he was, and she didn't feel at all at her best. Her hair was frizzing everywhere, her face was swollen, her eyes reddened. And she felt a heavy sadness inside her that not even meeting with him could dissipate. "Do you need anything?"

What a silly question, right now, in the face of tragedy. But it was all she could think of to say.

"I – I – well, I'm so shaken by what happened. I was actually going in search of tea."

"To the kitchen?" Mary asked.

He shook his head, making her notice how rumpled his hair was, sticking up and out, as if he'd been sleeping on it before being suddenly awoken. "When the housekeeper came around an hour ago to tell us about this death, she said there'd be a kettle set up in the parlor, just in case we were restless."

That made more sense. But it meant…

"So, you know what's happened?"

"I do," he said. "The police knocked on my door and asked me some questions. I feel – I feel terrible for my old friend, Sarah-Jane!"

Mary felt a new surge of surprise at the way he had referred to her.

"You knew her?" she asked. She guessed he had been to this manor house before. Maybe he'd met her then. Sarah-Jane would have been kind to him. She was kind to everybody!

But Gilbert's words, spoken softly in the semi-darkness of the corridor, surprised her.

"I knew her when she was at our local school. She was twelve years ahead of us and used to come in to help out when I was in my first year. When the teacher was sick, she even used to take classes, and supervise us little children. I've never forgotten that."

Mary felt a pang. So Sarah-Jane had also been in the teaching industry – well, sort of, just like her own mum had been. Maybe Sarah-Jane had also wanted to be a teacher and had tried to save up enough to do the course. That was one of Mary's goals. She wanted to save a nest egg that she could use to study and better herself, and teaching had been one of the ideas she'd had.

There was something strange about what Gilbert had said, and after a moment, Mary realized what it was.

She hadn't thought somebody wealthy, an upper-class person like Gilbert, would attend a local school. She'd have thought he would have had a private tutor, or a governess, or else, have gone to one of the fancy schools, the English public schools, where the wealthy folk went.

That was strange, but before she could think more about it, Gilbert continued.

"I heard that one of the housemaids found Sarah-Jane. That – that wouldn't have been you, would it?"

Unable to speak, Mary nodded.

Gilbert moved forward and for a moment, her heart did thump harder as she wondered if he might have been about to hug her. Or at any rate, clasp her hand, or do something comforting.

Then, as if he was rethinking whether this was appropriate behavior, he stood with his hands by his sides, and said, "I'm so very sorry about that. You must be extremely upset. Is somebody looking after you tonight?"

"I'll be alright," she reassured him bravely. "My friend was with me earlier, and the inspector has spoken to me, too."

"It's very troubling. Very. Are you sure you wouldn't like a cup of tea?"

She would. Under different circumstances, she would have loved to sit down with Gilbert for a cup of tea. But not now. Now, she was likely to burst into tears at any moment, and she didn't want to cry in front of him, and she was exhausted to the bone.

It was altogether the wrong time, and although a reckless voice inside her was saying, "You do want tea! You do!", the sensible voice in Mary's mind was saying, "Go to bed."

And she listened to the sensible voice.

"I have an early start tomorrow," she said, "and I'd better get some rest."

"Of course, of course," he said, with sudden understanding in his voice, as if he had forgotten what long, hard work her job involved. "I'll – well, I'll see you tomorrow morning, then. Hopefully, things will seem a bit better then."

"Good night," she said.

She walked on and took the staircase leading to her room. It was an effort not to look back, as she reached the bend in the corridor, but Mary managed.

Letting herself in, she slumped down on the bed.

Never, when she'd left this room, had she thought she'd be returning under these circumstances.

Mary pulled off her shoes and her dress, put on her nightgown, and wriggled in between the sheets, shivering for warmth, because this upstairs room was far away from any fireplaces, and kept chilly by the draft that filtered through the gap in the glass.

Sleep wouldn't come. She felt exhausted to the bone, but how could she allow herself to sleep in the wake of such unfairness?

They were sweeping this death under the carpet. It wasn't going to be investigated. For the sake of appearances, a killer would walk free?

For the sake of her friend, Mary knew she couldn't allow that. And for the sake of everyone else, too. Sarah-Jane had found something out, and that meant others could, too.

If nobody was going to seek the truth – then she would have to. And she had a clue – this person was 'not what he seems to be'.

To avenge her friend, she was going to have to tread on dangerous ground. A killer was hiding here, maybe even part of the elite Middlefield clan – and Mary was going to have to be brave enough to expose him.

CHAPTER ELEVEN

Jerking awake in the morning, Mary sat bolt upright, escaping from the chilly grasp of a nightmare. The details dissolved even as she tried to remember them, but it had definitely involved Inspector Braham, chasing her down a corridor, and yelling, "You'd better not poke your nose into this, Mary Adams, or you might find you meet with an accident, too!"

And then, she'd looked forward, and seeing a dark figure standing in front of her, brandishing a big steel bar.

It hadn't been a dream so much as a warning, then.

Breathing hard, she fought to put that troubling thought aside. This was a new day, the sky was beginning to lighten, and from downstairs she could hear the faint sounds of the manor house awakening – the scrape of coal from the fireplaces, the soft tread of footsteps, the hiss of the boiler that kept much of the household supplied with hot water.

The start of a new day. Mary promised herself, as she quickly dressed and got her unruly hair under control, that this was going to be the day she avenged Sarah-Jane's death.

To begin with, she was going to update Hannah on exactly what had happened.

As she put a hand on the doorknob, there was a soft knock from outside.

Great minds clearly thought alike. Hannah was at her door, dressed for work, her face anxious.

"Mary, I was so worried about you last night. What happened? I was scared that policeman would suspect you. I didn't see him for long, but he seemed rather strange," she blurted out as she slipped inside and Mary closed the door. "I was keeping my hopes up, though, since you and Sarah-Jane were good friends."

"Sit down." Mary patted the bed, and they sat down side by side.

"The policeman said it was accidental death," she then said, watching Hannah's face tauten with shock.

"Accidental? But that's impossible! How could she suddenly have died by accident?"

"She didn't," Mary explained. "She was worried about something last night. She wanted to tell me what it was. She said she'd found out a terrible secret, and she told me..." Mary lowered her voice, remembering the other thing that Sarah-Jane had mentioned, which was that walls had ears. "She told me 'he is not what he seems to be'."

Hannah's mouth dropped open. "Who isn't?"

"Unfortunately, she was killed before she could tell me that," Mary admitted.

"But – but that must have been why she wanted to meet you there. And this person – the one who wasn't who he seems to be – he must have followed her there on purpose!"

"That's exactly what I'm thinking."

Hannah glanced out of the small window, frowning at the grayish light that was breaking the darkness.

"Why doesn't the policeman think the same, then?"

"My theory is that one of the family has told him they don't want it to be murder." This was such a heretical statement to make under Middlefield Manor's very roof, that Mary dropped her voice to nothing more than a breath.

"How terrible!" Hannah gasped. "You think the police would do such a thing?"

"I think that policeman would," Mary clenched her hands together.

"So, what can we do?"

Feeling very glad that Hannah had used that all-important word 'we', which clearly meant she was prepared to help, Mary set out her plan. It was pretty simple, really. It took only five words to explain. Her mum had always said that the truth was easy to say.

"We find the killer ourselves."

Mary watched as a storm of emotions crossed Hannah's face.

Enthusiasm was first, followed by a flicker of doubt.

Then, naked fear showed itself for a few moments, an emotion that Mary understood, because after all, anyone who had killed Sarah-Jane because she'd learned his secret, wouldn't hesitate to kill again.

And finally, resolve was the expression that settled on Hannah's rosy-cheeked face.

"Let's do it," she said. "We need a plan, and we need to start today."

***

By the time they left the room, twenty minutes later, and with dawn now brightening the sky, they had sketched out what Mary hoped would be a workable plan. It all hinged on two things. Firstly, how much Hannah could find out by gossiping. She was better placed to do this because she had not been directly involved in any part of this tragic event. People might be willing to talk to her and share what they knew.

And since Mary and Hannah had only been at Middlefield Manor for a month, the chances were good that everyone knew more than they did.

Whatever they learned could help them.

And, talking of learning… Mary had a plan in mind that she hoped might allow her to retrace Sarah-Jane's steps yesterday, down to the very last footprint.

As soon as she walked into the kitchen, she headed for where Mrs. Inglethorpe was busy with her clipboard.

"Good morning, ma'am," she said politely.

Mrs. Inglethorpe was frowning down at the board, in the manner of somebody who now had too many jobs, and too few servants to complete them. That was exactly the predicament that Mary hoped she could help her solve.

"I'd like to volunteer to take over any of Sarah-Jane's tasks that you need help with," she said.

Mrs. Inglethorpe looked up at that, eyebrows raised as Mary continued.

"I know she was doing a lot of extra work and different chores, and if any of those need completing today, well, I thought it's the least I could do to offer," she said.

"Well, I must say, I was wondering who to assign to some of those," Mrs. Inglethorpe said. "You can follow her schedule today, then, and I'd be grateful for it. But there were some extra tasks she did yesterday that won't need doing today, so if there's a gap in the work, then you can go back and do your other jobs."

"I'll do that," Mary agreed.

So she hadn't got a full picture of what Sarah-Jane had done yesterday, but she would hopefully have most of it.

After some jottings on her clipboard, Mrs. Inglethorpe handed her a neatly penned schedule. Mary looked at it, her heart quickening. Somewhere in this timetable, a moment could have occurred that led to this murder. And now, she was going to have the chance to track this down.

First item on the agenda was an interesting one: *Clean Warwick's Room, Do Laundry.*

Warwick, the drunken ne'er do well, who'd been embroiled in that threatening conversation with Colin that she'd overheard yesterday. Were there secrets the brothers were keeping?

Or did she already know the secret, which involved Lady Ainsley and an affair?

"Is there anything I should know about Mr. Warwick Middlefield?" she politely asked Mrs. Inglethorpe, hoping to get the low down straight from one of the best sources.

"He's not been at the manor much, until recently, and he's usually a late riser," Mrs. Inglethorpe said. "And he's not the fondest of having his belongings tidied. However," she added in strict tones, "neatness is essential, as is good hygiene. So it will be up to you to find the right balance."

Mary had to admit, he sounded as difficult as his older brother Colin, just in a different way.

But a brother who'd left the family fold and struck out on his own, only to suddenly return, might have many secrets he was keeping.

He appeared to be the family's black sheep – but perhaps he was not what he seemed.

Making her way up to his rooms, which were not in the family's wing, but on a separate floor near the building's conservatory, she paused, listening outside.

A groan came from within the bedroom, followed by the thumping sound which Mary deduced was the sound of a hungover man getting out of bed.

"My head," she heard him mutter. "Damn it all, I need a vodka and tonic. Or else, a raw egg with a dash of brandy."

The raw egg concoction sounded vile, Mary had to admit. If he was feeling hungover enough to find that appealing, he must be in a bad way.

At any rate, it did, promisingly, sound as if he was soon going to leave his room in search of something to cure his headache, and that would give her the chance to snoop around inside. Not that she was going to do it obtrusively. Rather, she was just going to tidy.

More banging and clattering came from within, and then the door was wrenched open. Up close, and with stubble covering his face, hooded eyes, and rather pale cheeks, Warwick definitely did not look his best.

"Don't be too long in there," he told her gruffly. "I may be coming back to bed just now, so make sure it's made."

"I will do, sir," she replied in polite tones.

As soon as Warwick had staggered down the corridor, leaving a distinct whiff of alcohol in his wake, Mary headed inside.

Her eyes widened as she surveyed the room.

Untidy? That was an understatement. This room was a complete mess. She saw an empty whisky bottle on its side, lying on a pair of old socks. Two pairs of riding breeches lay entangled with each other on the floor, and a red hunting jacket was slung over the brass bedstead. The floor was littered with dirty shirts, riding magazines, and letters that were stained with food or drink, and on which he'd jotted inky notes.

Looking closer, on the pretext of tidying, she saw that one of them was a bill, from a bloodstock agent, for a large amount of money. It was overdue – by a couple of years! And the writer had requested "Mr. Middlefield's very urgent attention to this outstanding amount."

So as well as being messy, and rather rude to the help, Warwick also did not pay his bills?

Reminding herself that investigators should not pick sides, but must rather calmly survey the evidence, Mary put her personal feelings aside as she gathered up the dirty clothes.

This was a man who owed people money, who presumably was short of money or else very careless with it, and who was the third born.

She knew what that might mean. It might mean that Warwick Middlefield stood to inherit very little, if anything. Perhaps he'd been cut out of the will entirely as a result of his behavior, she theorized, picking up the empty bottle and putting it into her cleaning bucket, ready for removal downstairs.

Quickly, remembering that he might be back at any time, she made the bed.

It was as she was smoothing out the pillow carefully, that Mary heard something slip to the floor.

"What was that?" she muttered.

Something had tumbled down between the edge of the bed and the wooden headboard, and she worried that it had been something important, which Warwick might be angry if he missed. Now that she thought about it, she remembered he wore a number of rings on his fingers, chunky and silver, not very expensive looking but clearly important to him. If one of them had come off as he tossed and turned in his inebriated slumber, it could have fallen down.

She bent down and looked under the bed, but saw nothing there. No ring, no other objects, not even a speck of dust. Sarah-Jane had done a very thorough job, she thought, remembering her sadly all over again.

But perhaps she needed to look more closely. Something definitely had fallen down. If it hadn't landed on the floor, then where could it have gone?

Perhaps it had slipped into the mattress itself?

Pushing her hand down between the bed and the covers, wriggling it as far as she could get it, Mary felt something strange.

Where the sheet ended, there was a small cut in the mattress. She could feel its frayed edges. It was invisible to the eye, but it was there. Now, could she get her hand inside?

Twisting and turning so much that she gave herself a cramp in her thumb and had to stop for a moment to ease it, Mary forced her hand inside. What was this? This was a ring. And there was something else there, too, that she could feel beyond it.

Gritting her teeth and clamping two of her fingers together like scissors, Mary managed to draw the ring out from its odd hiding place.

She was right. This was one of the silver rings that Henry liked to wear, and so it must have fallen down as he tossed and turned this morning in a painfully wakeful state.

Now she was asking herself – what else was there?

Delving down with even more determination, feeling her wrist nearly crushed by the headboard, she managed to get her fingers around the object, and slowly and carefully, she drew it out.

Mary gasped in shock as she stared at it, unable to believe what she was seeing.

CHAPTER TWELVE

The object that Mary held in her now unsteady hand was the gold necklace that Lady Middlefield had said was missing! She'd turned her suite upside down in the hunt for it.

Mary gawped at it, wide-eyed. It had to be the same one. Lady Middlefield had described it in such detail. The hallmark on the clasp. The coat of arms on the pendant. It was identical down to the very last of the oval links. Heavy and gleaming in her hand, Mary knew there was no way this necklace could have slipped down into the mattress by accident.

Was anything else there?

Feeling cold shivers course down her spine, and startling guiltily as she heard the noise of footsteps passing by outside the window, Mary steeled herself, and her squashed wrist, for another foray into this secret compartment.

Her fingers touched something else heavy and gold.

And she drew out the ornamental elephant that Lady Middlefield had said went missing before Mary's arrival.

With her mind racing, Mary stared at the necklace and the elephant.

Only one person could have put them here – the man who was last in line to the family fortune, an acknowledged rake and spendthrift – and whose room Sarah-Jane had cleaned yesterday.

She must have found the selfsame items, and perhaps she'd confronted Warwick about them.

Or, maybe she hadn't had a chance. Maybe he'd walked in unexpectedly, and discovered her holding them.

With that in mind, Mary spun around, staring nervously at the door. A chillingly plausible scenario was presenting itself. She could imagine how Henry would have reacted. Jerked out of his usual semi-inebriated reverie, he would immediately have acted to protect his interests. After all, robbing your own family of valuables, which you could sell for your financial gain and possibly use to pay your outstanding bills, was definitely a secret that would have needed protecting.

And Sarah-Jane's rattled demeanor could have been because he'd threatened her with terrible consequences if she'd said a word. The first action of a guilty man would surely have been to do that.

Her first stop this morning, and she had answers. The killer was known to her now, but this secret was explosive, and if her theory was correct, Warwick Middlefield had already killed once, to protect it. Standing here, with these items in her now-clammy hands, Mary knew she was at terrible risk. She should put them back immediately.

Carefully, but working as fast as she was able to, she replaced the items, pushing them down in that gap in the mattress until they were invisible once again.

Now, what to do with the ring?

She decided to leave it on the dressing table and make sure to tell Warwick that she had found it under the bed. That would hopefully deflect his focus from her for as long as she needed.

Her heart was pounding. The next few minutes were going to be critical. The case was on the point of being solved – but she was at risk.

With lightning speed, she completed her quick tidy of the room, made the bed, and got things in order – enough so that Warwick would be happy with the state of his room, but not so much that he started wondering how thoroughly she'd checked his bed.

He came back just as she was finishing off, holding a half finished glass of a pale, strong looking drink with a slice of lemon in it. His face had a little more color now.

"Are you all done?" he asked brusquely. "I need to get some rest!"

Because he hadn't had any sleep last night, what with running around and killing people?

"Your ring was under the bed," Mary said calmly, clutching her bucket hard. "I left it on the dressing table for you."

"Under the bed?" He narrowed his eyes as if he was starting to put two and two together.

But by that time, Mary had managed to sidle unobtrusively to the door, and she slipped out as quickly as she could, speed walking along the corridor, the back of her neck prickling with the dread that he might call angrily after her at any moment.

It didn't happen, though. Armed with her cleaning equipment, and with her explosive new information, Mary made a safe getaway.

Breathlessly striding along the corridor, she knew that her very next stop needed to be Hannah. She had to share this information, and then they could decide what to do. Going to the police would be pointless.

The police, in the solid form of Inspector Braham, had already deemed this death accidental.

Lady Middlefield? Swallowing down her nerves, Mary wondered what her actual relationship with her lastborn son was like.

She didn't think that a son with a happy family relationship would steal from his mother. Therefore, she was guessing things between them were acrimonious.

Hopefully that might mean she and Hannah stood a chance of being believed, but a lot rested on how they approached this very delicate subject.

Seeing Hannah would be going about her normal routine today, and it was a fine day, that meant she would be outside, cleaning the first-floor windows at this time. Mary rushed to find her.

Heading out of the back door, she didn't dare to meet anybody's eyes, feeling as if the knowledge she now possessed about Warwick Middlefield was like a brand on her forehead that might be obvious to others. That at any moment, somebody might yell, "Hey, wait! You know something you're not telling, don't you?"

But no voices called out, as she headed through the back door, into the bright chill of the early morning. The sky was bright with a low, gleaming sunrise that she was sure had done nothing whatsoever to improve Warwick's hangover as it had blazed through the east windows.

She headed past the kitchen garden, a walled courtyard that was sheltered from the wind, and in which the cooks grew a variety of herbs, in pots around the sides of the courtyard, and in beds in the center.

It was always a fragrant place to pass through, and usually, Mary could never do it without stopping to touch at least one of the herbs. It was a sensory experience to rub a needle of rosemary between your fingers, and then smell that pungent, aromatic scent that brought such flavor and taste to the roast chicken, and the dishes of roast vegetables, that the cook made – and which they often got for leftovers in the staff pantry.

And the lemon verbena. How extraordinary that a herb could smell so – well, lemony. She'd asked the cook what it was used for, and the solid, gray-haired man, with his striped apron and his efficient demeanor, had told her that it was for summer fruit salads and frozen treats.

Then there was the basil, one of her favorites, and even though they weren't supposed to, Mary would sometimes pick a leaf and munch on it as she crossed the courtyard. The pungent flavor made her think of the tomato toppings, and the salads, and the cheese and pine nut breads, that it was combined with, creating nothing short of culinary poetry. In her opinion, anyway.

The big, green bed of sage was probably the most frequently used herb at the moment, with the winter menu featuring plentiful sausages, roast pork, roast turkey and goose, along with their stuffings and dressings.

This morning, Mary was too preoccupied to do more than inhale one appreciative breath as she quickly passed through that scenic herb garden and headed around to the south side of the manor house.

There was Hannah, on a step ladder, with her cleaning bottle and cloth, reaching up to make sure she cleaned every inch of the big ballroom windows.

"Hannah!" she hissed.

Turning around, Hannah quickly stepped down from the ladder. Her face was alight.

"Mary! I was going to come and find you as soon as I'd finished this. I found out something that might be important!"

"So did I," Mary replied, causing Hannah to look surprised.

Had they both stumbled upon the same secret, she wondered. Or, had Hannah discovered something else?

"What's yours?" Mary asked.

"Well!" Hannah leaned forward, conspiratorially. "I happened to pass by the stables on my way to do this chore."

Mary assumed that Hannah had detoured there intentionally, with the express aim of picking up information on those family members who enjoyed hunting and hacking out and carriage driving – which included a lot of the family.

"And?" Mary asked, sidling closer.

"And I happened to bump into Dickens, and he was in a chatty mood."

Mary remembered he'd been around the stables yesterday evening. He'd given her very valuable advice on finding Snowdon, the cat – advice that had shown a detailed knowledge of Middlefield Manor.

"What did he say?"

"He said that after dinner last night, there were two people from Middlefield Manor who were in the upstairs section of the hay barn.

Both very drunk and both *very* friendly with each other. He stayed there, out of the way, to watch them, in case they knocked anything over or started a fire, or upset the horses."

"Good heavens!" Mary said. She'd never thought such activities would form part of a head groom's duties. It wasn't just restless horses that kept him up late, it was people coming to the barn to roll in the hay!

"Who was it?" she asked, now intensely curious.

"Two people who should not have been doing such a thing together," Hannah replied, as if she was working up the courage herself to say what she needed.

"Go on – who?" Mary waited eagerly. With such a scandalous secret, she wondered if Hannah's suspect might even be the more likely killer.

She waited, in breathless trepidation, for Hannah to tell her the names.

CHAPTER THIRTEEN

"Well? Who was it?" Mary asked again, seeing that Hannah needed a moment to prepare herself for sharing what she'd learned. She could understand that. At the moment, Middlefield Manor was a threatening place – and one of their own had been murdered.

"It was Miss Janet, Colin Middlefield's wife," Hannah mumbled in a low voice. "And – and she was with – Warwick, Colin's younger brother!"

"What?" The word burst from Mary's lips – too loud. Hastily, she lowered her voice and looked around, worried that somebody had noticed. "The two of them?"

Warwick Middlefield was now doubly suspicious. He had not one but two dangerous secrets to hide. The only question, Mary decided, was which one they would start with when they approached Lady Middlefield.

"What are the details?" she asked.

"Well," Hannah continued. "They arrived there after dinner, and seeing as how they had a light with them, and Dickens didn't want them causing a fire, he kept an eye out until they'd finally gone – which was at around two a.m., he said. He removed the empty champagne bottles, and an item of underclothing which he didn't specify, at two-thirty."

Hannah's eyes were sparkling with excitement as she shared the scandal – but Mary's heart felt as if it had sunk all the way into her shoes.

"Oh, no!" she said. Hannah raised an eyebrow at the tone of her voice.

"I know, it's very shocking. You're probably wondering what to do about it, just like I am. So, while we think about it – what's the secret you found out?"

"It doesn't matter anymore," Mary had to force out the words. What a huge disappointment this was.

"What do you mean? Why not?"

"Because I thought Warwick Middlefield must be the killer. My secret, the one I found out, involves him too. He's stolen family jewelry and stashed it away in his mattress." Seeing Hannah's face tauten into shock, Mary quickly continued. "But your secret gives him an alibi! If he was up in the hay loft with Lady Janet, he couldn't possibly have killed Sarah-Jane."

Hannah blinked in surprise. "Oh, goodness! You're absolutely right about that! He couldn't have done it because he wouldn't have had the time."

Her brow furrowed. Clearly, she was doing her best to work out how this evil man might have managed to be in two places at once.

But Mary had already reluctantly resigned herself to the truth.

Though a thoroughly amoral character in many ways, and a person who was exceptionally rude to housemaids, Warwick's failings did not include being a killer.

The timing ruled it out.

Oh, dear. Now, she had the responsibility of keeping this dangerous secret, which at this point, she didn't feel ready to tell. That weighed uneasily on her heart.

Bitter though the disappointment was, Mary knew they would have to take it on the chin, and soldier on. At least there was one person in Middlefield Manor who they now knew it couldn't be. In fact – two. Warwick and Janet.

So, if nothing else, their pool of suspects was now smaller.

"Oh, dear," Hannah said. "I should have thought – when Dickens mentioned the timing – that obviously neither of them could have killed Sarah-Jane." Her face brightened again. "But don't worry. I'm sure I'll have more information soon because I'm going to be talking to the head butler when we have our tea break. We always end up in the pantry at the same time, and he's rather a gossip. This time, I'm going to encourage him to tell me everything he knows."

Mary double-checked her neatly written list of duties.

"I'm off to help out in the kitchens now," she said. "That was Sarah-Jane's job yesterday as well, and with extra guests here, I'm sure there's still a lot to do. Maybe the cook will have information."

Turning away, Mary realized that this was actually a very hopeful new angle.

After all, Sarah-Jane had been in the main kitchen when she'd buzzed Mary down. So whatever she'd learned could easily have happened right there.

***

The kitchens were a hive of activity when Mary hurried there. It was eight-thirty a.m., according to the clock on the wall, and that meant most guests would soon be making their way down for breakfast.

The cook, Mr. Rogers, was marching across the well scrubbed floor, holding a big steel tray on his shoulder.

"Fishcakes! Fishcakes!" he shouted. "Get them on the platters, quick. Our first guests are arriving in the dining room already! We need a plate of haddock delivered to Lady Mersey's room for the cat. You!" He pointed to the nearest butler, shoving the plate at him. "Take it!"

Grabbing a serving spoon, Mary got to work. The delicious-looking breakfast platters, of which there were three in total, contained a variety of tasty treats. As well as the fishcakes, there were slices of smoked ham, well browned sausages with their skins bursting open, deviled eggs, and a big bowl of baked beans, which were Mr. Rogers' specialty. He cooked them in a rich sauce that was bursting with flavors of tomato, herbs, and a hint of brown sugar. Mary hadn't liked baked beans much until she had started work at Middlefield Manor. Now, she realized how scrumptiously tasty they could be, when expertly prepared.

It was a breakfast feast, with the final touch added by baskets of toast and pastries on the side. The food preparation was a colorful and fragrant distraction, and Mary had to remind herself to keep on high alert and make sure her suspicions were not blunted by the aromas of this delicious meal.

After all, yesterday morning, Sarah-Jane had been helping out at this same breakfast preparation, and today, she was dead.

Although conversation was subdued, Mary realized that nobody except her was suspicious. All the others, from the snippets of talk she was picking up, seemed to think it had been a terrible accident.

"We must all be careful," one of the kitchen maids said, as the others nodded somberly.

"Watch yourself with that knife," another warned Mr. Rogers. "We need to be aware of accidents after last night."

"That, we do," one of the assistant cooks echoed from behind Mary, in her lilting Irish accent.

"Too sad and tragic," another said. "Could happen to any of us, in a careless moment."

"What does Martin want for his breakfast?" one of the housemaids asked as she rushed in. "He was feeling poorly again last night."

Mr. Rogers glanced up, frowning.

"Somebody needs to go and ask him that." His gaze fell on Mary. "You go, won't you? Tap on his door and find out what he feels like."

She hadn't had much to do with Martin, but felt sorry for him. It must be terrible to feel queasy and poorly all the time after recovering from such a serious accident, and it seemed that nobody had been able to figure out why.

But before she could agree, a voice rang out from the doorway.

"Oh, he's already told me what he needs, just like yesterday. And I'll take it up to him. It's the least I can do for my poor cousin! Bringing him his meals, on the days I spend here, is a way of making up to him for this terrible affliction he suffers from!"

The speaker was somebody that Mary had seen last night, going into dinner, but whom she didn't know by anything other than sight. He was clearly a cousin, though. And there was something about his tone – it was syrupy sweet.

The man himself looked suave and well groomed, with light brown hair slicked back with so much pomade it glowed, and wearing a blue velvet jacket.

Mary distrusted anyone who was that syrupy sweet. It didn't ring true. Why was he so concerned about Martin? What was his reason for wanting to take him his meals whenever he was here – which sounded as if it was often?

Maybe if she'd just been helping out in the kitchen, she would have overlooked it. But she wasn't – she was helping out in the kitchen while figuring out who killed Sarah-Jane. And for that reason, she needed to be suspicious of everything.

"Thanks, Mr. Barry." The cook nodded politely. "As usual, then."

So that was the cousin's name, and the cook didn't seem suspicious of him. That meant this was a frequent occurrence. Although, the cook was probably too busy at breakfast time to worry about such details, and not to be anything but grateful for some help.

Since the fishcakes were now all on the platters, which the serving maids were taking through, Mary decided that she was going to temporarily abandon her duties. Instead, she was going to subtly watch what this cousin did.

He took a plate from the rack, with the ease of familiarity, and quickly scooped up a selection of food from the platter that remained in the kitchen. A fishcake, a sausage, and a surprisingly large portion of those juicy, gravy-infused beans. Then, he whisked a piece of toast onto the plate, grabbed a knife and fork, and headed quickly out.

"What's going on?" Mary muttered, sidling over to the door where he'd disappeared. Where was he going? That wasn't the way to Martin's room. Why was Barry heading in a different direction?

She tiptoed after him. He wasn't going to the corridor that led to the bedrooms at all. Instead, he was detouring – and to her surprise, she saw he was making his way to a retaining wall, behind which was a narrow downstairs staircase.

This must lead to one of the other cellars Sarah-Jane had told her about!

Had she discovered it yesterday, while following the cousin down here?

Now feeling intent on finding the truth, she headed after him, watching as he quickly descended the winding stairway, plate in hand.

Mary tiptoed down after him, walking carefully. The cellar seemed to have been used for storing wood, and there were some loose pieces of wood lying on the stairs, as if someone had made a quick trip this morning to get some, and dropped a couple of sticks along the way.

Barry had been able to avoid them, but her skirt might easily brush this wood off a stair. She didn't want to make a sound – but she did want to get close enough to see what he was doing.

The click of a switch told her he'd turned on the light. Now, the darkness down there was less shadowy, and she could see a faint glow from beyond the wall.

He was rustling around down there, as if he was opening something. How could she possibly see more, without being noticed in turn?

Maybe if she looked through this gap in the stones?

The first gap showed her nothing, but there was a bigger gap further down. She edged down two more stairs, and then looked again.

Catching her breath, clutching at her skirt, Mary realized this gap in the stone wall gave her a narrow, but clear view into the cellar itself. With the light on, it was easier to see, and she stared hard.

He had the plate set down on a plank. And now, he was rummaging in his pocket.

What was he taking out?

Mary stared, frozen, as he unfolded a twist of paper and carefully sprinkled a white powder all over the surface of those baked beans.

Her heart started drumming, rapidly.

She couldn't believe her eyes, but the evidence was clear. For reasons she couldn't understand, Barry was poisoning his cousin Martin. It was poison in that twisted-up paper! It had to be. It wasn't anything good, being applied to the food down here, away from all watching eyes, in stealth and secrecy.

This could have been the exact scene that Sarah-Jane witnessed yesterday.

"He is not what he seems." Well, Barry clearly was not.

And, as she had that thought, a fold of Mary's skirt dropped down from the tight grasp she'd been holding it in, and the fabric brushed against a sliver of wood.

It went tumbling down the staircase, making a noise as loud as any she'd ever heard. It caused Barry's head to jerk around, instantly.

Mary froze for one terrible moment too long. Pure terror surged through her, temporarily paralyzing the sensible part of her brain which was screaming at her, "Run! Now!"

Mary didn't run, and in another second, there was no time to.

Because Barry had erupted from the cellar and was standing in the doorway, staring up at her.

CHAPTER FOURTEEN

Breathing rapidly, Mary stared down at Barry the poisoner, feeling her life flash before her eyes as scenarios – none good – played out.

If he didn't kill her now, he'd come for her later. And what evidence did she have? He could throw the food away, say he'd spilled it, deny this completely, and it would be his word against hers.

But then, Mary realized something strange.

Barry was looking just as terrified as her.

His face was pale. His weak chin was quivering. He looked, frankly, horrified. And that gave Mary the courage she needed to speak up. After all, how could she do otherwise when such a terrible crime was being committed?

"You were putting something on Martin's food," she accused him.

He gulped visibly. "I was not!"

"I saw you and you were!" she said. No backing down now.

"What ridiculousness. I came down here to get – just to get something I'd forgotten here. While on the way to Martin's room."

"What had you forgotten? Your poison powder?" Mary's anger was overriding her fear. "You put it on his beans! It's probably sunk in by now."

"No! I love my cousin. I bring him his meals often. I'm as sorry as anybody that he's ill."

"You're causing that illness! Why? What do you gain from it?"

"Nothing! And you're wrong."

"In that case," Mary thought of a clever solution, "why don't you eat the food? Seeing it's so safe? You shouldn't have a problem doing that. Go on! Take a big mouthful of those beans. I dare you to!"

"I – er –" His voice tailed off. He'd run out of argument, she realized, with a flash of triumph. Even in this precarious situation, a small victory was something.

"Don't say anything," he whispered. There was a begging tone to his voice. "Please! I didn't - I didn't mean for it to go this far. It's just a bit of arsenic, that's all."

"A bit of arsenic!" Mary's voice rose incredulously, and he waved his hands at her, looking stressed.

"Please, not so loud! I thought it would just – just make him ill enough that I could benefit from the clause in the will that Aunt Middlefield wrote in after he had the hunting accident. It says if the second son is not sound in body or mind and is confined to the manor house with illness, then the holiday home in Shropshire and the apartment in London will go to the firstborn cousin. I mean, it's not my fault that Lady Middlefield hates Warwick so much that she'd put me in the will instead of him. I just thought I'd try to keep Martin feeling – er – a little unwell, because that apartment in London is very nice."

"But that's appalling! You could easily have killed him, and you might still do just that."

She marched down the stairs. Righteous anger fueled her now as she grabbed the plate. She had intended to pour the beans out onto the floor, but rethought her actions as she lifted it. What if a harmless mouse got sick from it?

"I - I'd so appreciate you remaining quiet about it. I mean, I can offer you money, a jeweled bracelet? Do you like jewels? What's your favorite jewel?" he asked in a wheedling tone.

"I don't have a favorite, and don't like any of them."

He looked hurt. "Are you sure? What's your name, by the way?"

"My name's Mary. And that's not the point. The point is that I don't want any gifts from you!"

Experience had taught her that jewelry in this house didn't always belong to the people who had it in their possession. She wasn't about to accept any gift from a poisoner, though, whether it belonged to him or not.

"Mary, may I at least have your word, as a – as a housemaid, that you will keep this to yourself?"

Time to bargain with him, as best she could.

"I won't say anything for now, but that's on condition that you answer my question truthfully," she said.

"Your question? I'll try. What question?"

"Did Sarah-Jane see you yesterday?" she demanded.

"Did who? Who's she?" he asked. The note of puzzlement in his voice seemed genuine, but Mary reminded herself that a cold-blooded killer didn't have to know someone's name in order to hit them over the head with an iron bar.

"One of the housemaids. The one who met with an accidental death last night." Mary made sure her voice was loaded with meaning, but the significance seemed to bypass Barry completely.

"No, nobody saw me yesterday," he admitted, crestfallen. "But Martin also didn't eat his beans. I think – well, I think he's starting to suspect me anyway. My plan might not be working as well as I'd thought. This was really my last chance. Today. The arsenic's almost finished."

He showed her the twist of paper. Sure enough, only a few grains of the white powder remained. But he could get hold of more poison if he was determined to keep poor Martin bedridden – or kill him off completely.

"Where were you last night?" she demanded. She needed him to account for his time to prove he wasn't the killer. Now that the tables had turned and he seemed afraid of her, she wasn't just going to take a stammering denial at face value.

"I was at dinner. I went to the smoking room with some of the others."

"And after that?"

"After that, I went to bed. I woke up when there was that commotion. When the maid fell over and hit her head on a tractor or some such issue? Then everyone started making a noise and I got out of bed."

He hadn't had any witnesses, and Mary was going to have to use her own judgment here. But as she assessed the way he was speaking now, compared to the way he'd spoken when he'd said it wasn't poison in the food, she thought there was a big difference in his demeanor. He hadn't seemed guilty now. When he'd spoken about the food, and he'd been lying, his face had twitched, and he'd kept on lifting a hand to rub his chin. Now, neither of those physical tics were obvious.

She still wasn't entirely sure about him, but the deciding factor for her was how afraid he'd been to be found out. He'd been scared and looking to bribe her into silence. That was a world away from the emotion that would prompt somebody to commit murder. So, she was going to keep searching for now.

Mary felt instinctively that the killer was hiding elsewhere in the manor, and that if she pursued Barry, she'd be wasting her time.

She took the plate from him, turned, and marched up the stairs. Then, she carried it the whole way back to the kitchen.

She'd intended to go straight into the scullery and wash every one of those beans down the sink. Hopefully, that would dilute the poison enough that it wouldn't hurt anybody else.

But as she'd turned into the passage that led to the kitchen's side door, she heard a voice from behind her, coming from the main corridor.

"Mary!"

Spinning around so suddenly that the beans nearly slid right off the plate, she stared in consternation.

It was Gilbert, hurrying toward her with a worried expression on his handsome face.

CHAPTER FIFTEEN

What a moment to meet up with Gilbert MacLeod! Mary tried to suppress a surge of panic at the unfortunate timing of the situation. Last night had been bad enough, bumping into him when she was upset and tear-stained and in no condition to speak to anyone coherently.

But this felt even worse. Now, here she was, in the middle of an investigation, and carrying a plate of poisoned beans back to the kitchen!

It was becoming very hard to come across the way she wanted to, in front of Gilbert, when their meetings were occurring at such inopportune moments.

Inopportune was a word that her schoolteacher mum had found it difficult to explain to her, but Mary was understanding that definition perfectly, now that she was living and breathing it.

"Gilbert," she said, moving her thumb just a little so it didn't touch the beans. She wanted *nothing* to touch those beans.

"Mary." He moved forward, speaking quietly. Surprised, she saw how worried he was looking. His dark hair was wilder and wavier than usual. His eyes looked reddened, as if he hadn't slept well, and he looked paler than she remembered. At any rate, those appealing freckles were more visible – if she herself hadn't been so preoccupied, she would have paid them better attention. What a missed opportunity it was.

"I'm worried. That whole business last night – well, you might think it strange of me, but I've been wondering if it wasn't an accident. It just seems so unlikely. But yet, the alternative is unthinkable. Anyway, I wanted to discuss it with you."

Her eyebrows rose. He was right on the money there.

"I think Sarah-Jane was deliberately murdered," she muttered to him. "And I'm going to find out who did it."

There was a short, loaded silence.

"Mary, no, please!" Gilbert said. "I came to warn you, because surely this could get very dangerous? I – well, I don't want you in harm's way. I want you to stay safe. That's what I came to tell you. I feel like I know you as – as a friend. And as a friend, I'm very concerned for you."

He was worried now? Mary wondered how much more worried he'd be if he discovered that she'd followed a poisoner down to the cellar, caught him in the act, and was even now clutching the spoils of that encounter?

"Sarah-Jane was a friend of mine, too," Mary said. "And I'm not going to leave it alone. She was a good person, and she found something out that got her killed."

Gilbert frowned. "But if you find the same thing out, you could be killed, too."

Mary hesitated. "It's a possibility, but I can't let that hold me back."

"Won't the police investigate it?"

She shook her head, causing the now congealing beans to wobble. "The police think it was an accident, and that inspector is not going to change his mind. He's been persuaded, somehow, that this is what happened."

She could hear the contempt in her own voice. There was no respect at all due to people like Inspector Braham.

Gilbert pressed his lips together. "Oh, dear," he said. "You know, I've heard of this happening in the past, when these powerful families decide they don't want any scandal."

There was a strange note of contempt in his voice when he said 'powerful' that she didn't understand. He was from a powerful, highborn family too. His family owned lots of land and must have done for centuries. She didn't understand why he was speaking that way.

And unfortunately, she couldn't agree to what he was pleading with her to do.

"So you see," she said softly. "The police aren't going to look into it, it's been deemed accidental, and if I don't try to find out what happened, then nobody might ever know, and that would be hugely unfair."

"What if the killer murders again, and targets you?" Gilbert asked. "Isn't there another way to do this? Somebody else who could try to find out who's less – less exposed than you are?"

"What if the murderer decides he likes killing, and starts targeting others anyway?" she countered. "Nobody is safe here until he's found."

Gilbert sighed. "I can see you're set on this. Just please, take care. I was supposed to leave this morning, but I still haven't had a chance to speak to Colin yet, so I'll be here a while longer. Please, if there's anything you need, or you feel you're in danger – call me, or come and find me, or alert me somehow. Will you promise that?"

Despite the fact she'd just been arguing with him, and was still holding a plate of congealing poisoned beans, Mary couldn't help but feel a surge of warmth inside her as she saw the honesty in his eyes.

He was seriously concerned. And she had no doubt that if the worst happened and she did end up in danger, he would do his utmost to help.

"I promise," she said, and he nodded, looking a little less stressed than he had done.

"Gilbert!" A voice called out from down the corridor, and he quickly headed in that direction, causing her to feel disappointed. With the urgency of his warning out of the way, there might have been a chance to talk to him about other things.

She wanted to know why his attitude about the upper classes was so strange and uncharacteristic, and she promised herself that the next time she saw him, she would ask.

Right now, though, she was getting rid of every one of these beans.

Hurrying through to the scullery, she turned on the tap in the sink, tipped the rest of the food into the trash, and washed every one of those poisoned baked beans down the plughole, shivering as she did so. What a horrible man Barry was! And how deluded and greedy – for the sake of a holiday home and a London apartment, this already wealthy man had stooped so low?

Once the baked beans were all gone, and the plate was clean, Mary hastily returned to her breakfast post. Although it wasn't officially part of her working day, the first thing she did was to take a fresh plate from the stack on the shelf, and dish out a small, but unpoisoned, selection of food – light, but appetizing – toast, butter, a fishcake, and also some beans straight from the pot, although they gave her the shivers after what had happened.

She took the plate through to the dining room and peeked inside, managing to catch the eye of a footman who was standing nearby.

"I wonder if you could take this plate up to Martin Middlefield?" she asked. "He's waiting for his breakfast. Please don't let anyone tamper with it along the way – and could you stay outside the door until he's finished it? It's very important that he eats it alone and without being disturbed."

The footman's eyebrows rose, but he didn't ask any questions, and Mary guessed he believed this odd request probably originated from Martin himself.

“I’ll do that,” he agreed, taking the plate.

With Martin’s breakfast safely on its way, Mary returned to the kitchen. Her duties now consisted of washing up the cooking items, bringing dishes through from the dining room, and mopping the kitchen floor to a state of sparkling cleanliness.

Only when that was done, did she look at Mrs. Inglethorpe’s list again to see what her next chore was.

The moral dilemma of what to do about Martin Middlefield was still weighing on her shoulders. There was no guarantee that the cowardly Barry wouldn’t continue poisoning him once he’d gotten hold of more arsenic. She needed to warn him – but how?

That was troubling her mind as she turned back to the list of duties in her pocket. It seemed that life at Middlefield Manor was suddenly becoming intensely complicated. With everyone’s secrets now being exposed, she was having to make some hard decisions that wouldn’t usually be a housemaid’s responsibility at all – like how to warn poison victims!

But for now, her next task was taking her to the other side of the manor house.

According to this neatly penned note, the tutor who usually looked after the Middlefield grandchildren, and helped them with their education, was ill for the week, and so Sarah-Jane had been tasked with supervising a study period for the youngest grandson.

His name was Ferdinand, and if Mary remembered correctly, he was about seventeen years old. She'd seen him in passing, and he had always greeted her politely. He seemed like a nice young man, and she couldn't possibly envision him being a killer at all. Surely it was impossible?

However, it was her duty to go and look after him, and maybe this session would be helpful to her.

After all, she might be a housemaid now, but she had aspirations to become something else one day. This might be an important learning experience for her. Supervising this young man might even be the first step in a teaching career.

Despite the circumstances, it was an exciting opportunity! If she did it well, perhaps she could stand in for the tutor regularly.

Passing the drawing room, she glanced at the small clock that stood on the mantelpiece, seeing that she was, in fact, still fifteen minutes early. The tutoring session which she was supervising started at eleven, and it was still only a quarter to.

It would be impolite to arrive so early, and she didn't want to start something so important on the wrong foot. Mary slowed all the way down to a dawdle, realizing that even the slowest walk would get her there far too early.

What she needed was something else to do in the time.

A thought came to her, so scandalously daring that she banished it immediately, feeling her cheeks grow hot at the very idea.

But the thought refused to be banished. It returned to her, and this time, more strongly.

"While Lady Middlefield is down at breakfast and her assistant is out of the adjoining office, why not have a look and see what's in that chest in her bedroom, the one that she guards so closely? Because that's a secret, too. And even if Lady Middlefield didn't kill for it herself – maybe somebody else found out about it, and they did."

Once that little voice had started whispering to her, there was no way Mary was able to silence it. Dangerous as it was to snoop in the lady's rooms, this was going to be the best time of day to do it, and if she didn't find out, she might just be allowing a killer to walk free.

As if she had no control of them at all, Mary found her legs turning in the direction of Lady Middlefield's wing. Climbing the staircase, she knew that she was now committed to what she was going to do.

If she was discovered – this might mean not just the end of her job, but of her life.

CHAPTER SIXTEEN

"Well, Mary," she whispered to herself, trying to keep up her morale at this terrifying time, "you just need to keep your wits about you and your ears open. There's no reason why anyone should see you here, and if they do, you have plenty of places you can hide."

After all, she'd cleaned Lady Middlefield's rooms for a month now. She knew about the space behind the dresses in the wardrobe that she dusted every day, where she could crouch down out of sight if needed. And she knew how easily items could be lost behind the high backed, low legged double seat next to the fireplace. A scarf had fallen down there and been totally invisible. Alright, so she was a lot bigger than a scarf – but still, it was a solid sofa.

Then there was the bathroom which was right next door, with its enormous, claw footed bath. That was certainly a hiding place where, if you lay down flat inside the bath, you'd be invisible to anybody walking in.

So there were options available. The fact that she didn't like any of them, or have faith in them standing up to a basic search, was not something she needed to worry about now. What she needed to worry about was looking inside that chest.

Mary tiptoed up to the door and tapped on it very lightly.

She waited, holding her breath, for any sound from inside, but heard nothing. No clink of china to suggest that Lady Middlefield was having her breakfast in her rooms, instead of in the drawing room. No rustle of paper to indicate that her assistant was busy at his desk in the annex room. Nothing at all.

So, gathering her courage, Mary turned the handle, stepped inside, and closed it again behind her.

The enormous room was neat and clean and totally silent. Sunshine streamed in through the window, making the air feel warm, and a hint of the lady's lilac perfume to be discernible.

Firstly, she glanced anxiously into the annex to check whether Howard was at work. He wasn't. His desk was neat, with the papers squared off. Clearly, everyone was still downstairs, lingering over coffee, and bidding farewell to the birthday guests. She'd chosen her time well.

Tiptoeing across the carpet, Mary felt guilty – like an intruder or a burglar. She'd never walked into this room with nefarious motives before. It felt wrong to be doing this – but if she didn't, then how would she ever find out what she needed to?

Killing was wrong too, she reminded herself. And so was covering up a crime. Both those wrongs had been committed under the roof of Middlefield Manor. All she was trying to do was expose those wrongs.

She walked past the card table, taking a glance at the abandoned patience game, which hadn't yet been tidied away. For someone who loved playing cards, Lady Middlefield was surprisingly bad at them. It was a trait that her granddaughter had clearly inherited, only with a piano instead of cards.

That flicker of humor gave her the resolve she needed to pass the card table, which somehow felt like a psychological barrier, and make her way cautiously to the chest, resting beside the crisply made bed.

Breathing in deeply, she moved forward and touched it, resting her hands on the lid, just as she'd done that day when Lady Middlefield had shouted at her so sharply.

There was clearly a very closely guarded secret inside this chest, and now, Mary's only regret was that she hadn't thought to come in here and open this lid earlier. If she had, then by now, she might know what the reason for the murder was.

She curled her fingers under the lid and opened it.

The first thing she realized was that a faint smell of roses was in the air. And staring down as the lid opened, she saw that the contents of the trunk were topped with a pile of pink rose petals – ancient and dried, but still with a subtle fragrance about them, as if it had been trapped in here for a long, long time.

Resting the lid gently against the wall, Mary peered down, her heart beating fast. But, as she made sense of the items that were neatly piled below the rose petals, shock suffused her. This wasn't what she'd expected to find here. Not at all.

The items were baby's clothes. A pink dress, tiny woolen shoes, a white knit cap, and a few soft blankets. There was even a faded piece of paper that seemed to be a christening invitation, but now that she was making sense of these contents, Mary couldn't bring herself to look at it.

This was a secret she'd never expected – the existence of a daughter. So Lady Middlefield hadn't just had sons. She'd also had a girl who, from the contents of the trunk, must have died when she was very young. That was why this imperious lady had kept the memory of her daughter's possessions close to her, right by her bedside, for what must surely have been decades.

That was so sad that Mary felt her chest hiccup with a sob. She'd only known this grand dame at this stage of her life – when she was elderly and crotchety and discontented. Now she had a sudden vision of her earlier life, as a young woman with hopes and dreams, with a family, and with a precious daughter who had died.

Lady Middlefield was not what *she* seemed, and the contents of the chest had proven it.

"I'm so sorry," Mary whispered. She felt thoroughly guilty now at having snooped, finding nothing incriminating, but only a treasured memory of the saddest loss.

She gently replaced the lid and patted the top of it, sending a loving wish to the memory of that little daughter and the mother's grief.

And then, she was jerked right out of her somber state of mind by a sound she'd not wanted or expected to hear.

Brisk footsteps were approaching the bedroom door.

Her window for being in here alone had abruptly passed. Somebody was about to open this bedroom door, and then they'd find her here – inside, and crouching over the forbidden trunk.

Panic flooded her, but only for a moment. Then, thankfully, her brain sprang into action and told her to hide, hide, hide!

Not even knowing if she'd be able to get there in time, Mary jumped to her feet and bolted across the room, heading for the wardrobe.

CHAPTER SEVENTEEN

It felt like everything was happening in a dreadful slow motion.

As Mary's hand grasped the wardrobe door, she heard the doorknob of Lady Middlefield's bedroom turn with its customary soft click.

As Mary wrenched open the wardrobe door, she saw the bedroom door swing open.

And then, she jumped inside, closing the door as fast as she could, nearly bringing the whole rail of dresses down as she stumbled in the sudden darkness. That would be a catastrophe. If whoever had come into the room was to hear such a crash, it would all be over.

By wedging her elbow desperately against the wardrobe's side and bracing her legs, she managed to keep her footing without moving any of the dresses or dislodging the rail.

Trying not to breathe at all, she stepped back, easing herself between the dresses. With silk and satin and lace brushing over her face and hands, she got herself down into a crouching position and stayed as still as possible.

Even though her heart was hammering so loudly she was surprised the whole wardrobe wasn't shaking, the rest of her was totally silent. And in the silence, she could pick up noises from outside.

She'd hoped that it might be one of the housemaids coming in to check for dirty glasses, or bring in clean linen. As she made sense of the noises, though, her hopes were dashed. This was no housemaid. This was the assistant, Howard. Now that the thundering of her own blood in her ears had diminished, she could make out his voice. He was humming to himself softly, as he liked to do when he was settling down for a session at his desk.

His desk was in the annex of the bedroom, and it faced the doorway.

He never closed the annex's door. She had never seen it closed, and she hadn't heard it close now. It was open, and that meant she could not get past. If she tried, he'd see her. There was absolutely no way she could creep past that open door without him noticing. And if he noticed, then it would all be over. She would have to explain why she was coming out after having been in here alone. The longer she waited, the worse it would be.

But even if she went out now and said she'd just popped in to check for dirty dishes, it would already be too late. Already, it was too long a time to have spent in this room, and that excuse would no longer wash, especially since Lady Middlefield liked to be in attendance when the housemaids did their cleaning.

With a rising sense of horror, Mary realized she was well and truly trapped. Howard might work for a couple of hours. And she, in just five minutes, was due to supervise Ferdinand at his studies.

"Well, you really have gone and complicated things," Mary chastised herself, hoping that a good old-fashioned scolding would dislodge the sense of doom she felt – the sense that there was no way out of the situation at all.

Already, her legs were starting to burn from the effort of holding herself still in that crouched pose. Gently, she eased herself down onto a knee. That, in turn, immediately began to ache and quiver.

Could she get to a window?

In the pitch darkness of the wardrobe, illuminated only by the faint light that emanated through the keyhole, Mary thought about that. There were three windows in the room. Two of them were out of sight of the annex. The problem was that Lady Middlefield hated the wintry air, and forbade any windows to be opened. Never had she seen any of those pretty, Gothic windows open as much as a crack.

That meant the latches were likely to be extremely stiff. Experience had already taught her what happened to things in these old, stately homes when they weren't regularly moved or used. They stuck, and rusted, in a flash. She could imagine the squeal of the latch mechanism and the shriek of hinges that would accompany her efforts.

It was very unlikely that she'd manage to get out before the assistant came rushing through, asking her what on earth she was up to. And being stuck, with her backside on one side of the sill and her shoulders on the other, would be a difficult situation to innocently explain away. Impossible in fact.

And even if, by some miracle, she was able to get out of the window in time, this was a high-set, second-floor room. How was she planning to get down to ground level? Shimmy down the creeper?

Mary rolled her eyes at the folly of her own thoughts. There was no way out of the window. Even Snowdon the cat had scorned the idea of using it.

But thinking of Snowdon gave Mary a sudden idea.

Clever Snowdon had found a secret passage at the back of the wardrobe, and he'd gone in there to have the most private nap ever.

Now, she was wondering if that had been the only room with a secret passage attached to it. After all, Dickens had said that this was an ancient manor house with lots of hiding places where, in past years, valuables had been squirreled away to hide them from sight.

And thanks to her experimentation in Lady Mersey's room, she knew how the wardrobe mechanism worked.

How noisy had it been, she wondered, as she felt over the wood with hands that were suddenly damp. It had been somewhat noisy. But not very noisy. It had been a click and a rattle.

How had she done it? In the pitch dark, it was very difficult to work out exactly where she'd found that panel in the other wardrobe. Had it been here?

Mary thought it had been round about here. And as she felt, her heart sped up as her fingers touched a familiar clasp in the wood.

This was the same!

This wardrobe, too, had a secret passage and if she could get into it, maybe it led somewhere. Even leading into another room would be enough to save her.

She took a deep breath. It might not even move. Or if it moved, it might make such a noise that the assistant would instantly come running.

Sending up a little prayer, Mary undid the clasp and pressed on the wood, to slide the panel aside.

CHAPTER EIGHTEEN

The wood slid back. To Mary's ears, the noise seemed deafening. The click it made seemed like it resounded the whole way around Middlefield Manor, and the shift of the wood sounded as bone-rattling as an earthquake.

She froze, but Howard didn't call out, "Who's there?" and in fact, she heard no movement from the annex at all.

Maybe the closed wardrobe door, and the insulation of all those dresses, had muffled the sound. At any rate, the panel had moved, and she now needed to find out if she could wriggle through it.

She felt the sides of the gap, which was about two feet by three feet in diameter, the same as the other one had been. A narrow gap, but definitely big enough to crawl through.

Wishing she had a light with her, and fervently hoping there were no spiders lurking in these pitch black depths, Mary reached out a hand, touching the smooth, chilly stone wall beyond the wardrobe, feeling the shape of the passage. She eased herself into it, first her hands, then her body, and finally her legs, stepping carefully through the gap so that her feet rested on the stone floor. Exploring the space with her hands, she realized that it was now a little higher. The gap in the wardrobe had been small, but the tunnel beyond was about five feet high, though very narrow. It was high enough for her to stand, even though she'd be in a stooped position.

She'd need to keep her hands in front of her, or she'd risk walking into something, or else getting a nasty bump on the head if that roof suddenly lowered.

With her hands raised defensively at head level, feeling in front of her with her toes in case the ground suddenly disappeared from under her and she fell into a pit, Mary shuffled forward. One step, then another. It was a strange and disconcerting feeling to know that she was stumbling blindly along in an actual secret corridor, like a catacomb.

That brought a shiver to her spine, because now, her mind was imagining something worse than spiders. Bones.

What if she suddenly stepped into a big pile of them? What if the hand in front of her face touched a grinning skull?

Mary swallowed down her panic, giving her imagination a severe telling off for having produced this scenario at such a time. Of course, there would be no bones here, she firmly repeated. No bones at all. And why was she so sure?

She was sure because the passage didn't smell musty at all. It didn't smell in the least like somewhere that people had died. In fact, it smelled familiar in rather a pleasant way, although a way that her brain was battling to place.

What could she smell in this passage, she wondered, taking yet another step forward. It was impossible to be sure in the disorienting darkness, but she thought the passage might be veering to the right. If that was the case, then she would be walking beyond Lady Middlefield's rooms.

Tea!

Once her nose had accurately identified the smell, it was unmistakable and most definitely reassuring. A secret passage that smelled of tea leaves could surely not be a deadly place. At any rate, this was making Mary feel better about this precarious and uncharted journey.

Now there was a corner in the corridor ahead of her, but there wasn't a choice of ways. It just felt as if the corridor had widened out.

Exploring ever so carefully with her toes and fingertips, she realized that it had widened out into a small room. There was no way out of the room. No door, no wooden section. Just the room itself, probably two yards square, and then the narrow passage continuing on. So the room must be an extremely well-hidden store room. It was big enough for a person to have hidden here. Images, far back in history, of kings and traitors and secret keepers hiding away, crowded her mind as she headed on, wondering where the rest of the passage would lead her.

After a few more tentative yards, her outstretched hands hit a solid wall. It was stone – but was it a dead end? That would be a terrible disappointment. Surely it couldn't be? She crouched down and felt carefully, exploring it all over with her fingertips, flinching as she really did hear something scuttling away, just a few inches from her face.

And as she explored, she felt the same thing she'd felt on the other side. There was a wooden panel here. So this passage now led to the back of another cupboard, although she had no idea at all which room it was in. She wasn't sure which direction the corridor had led her in.

It wouldn't be the guest rooms, she was certain of that, which might mean it would be one of the family's rooms.

Holding her breath, she listened. No sound from outside.

Would it be possible to open this panel from inside? For a few moments she tried, but all her frantic poking and prodding brought no results, and she was starting to despair.

And then, she felt it.

A small lever all the way on the right of the doorway. This must move somehow. If she could push it, or pull it, or somehow tweak it, then it might undo the clasp on the other side, and allow her to open the panel.

Mary pulled the lever. It didn't budge.

She pulled it harder, and then, with the same click and shift, the clasp loosened, and the panel opened obediently, just as if it had last been used yesterday.

Beyond was a faint blob of light. It came from a keyhole.

She was in another wardrobe. And now, she had to get out – and safely through whoever's bedroom this was.

It belonged to a man, that was clear. There were no lacy, satiny garments here. As she climbed through the gap, she kicked over a pair of long leather riding boots. They tumbled onto their side with a clatter, causing Mary to freeze. Would anyone hear that?

Nobody flung open the wardrobe door, so after a short but heart-pounding pause, she continued climbing through.

A riding jacket, a few pairs of breeches, a few dinner jackets, and some starched shirts. She could see the array of clothing dimly through the light the keyhole provided.

Now, she was the whole way through. Could she close this gap again?

She pushed at the wooden panel, and after some wiggling, her efforts were rewarded, and it slid jerkily into place again.

Where was she? And would she be able to get out of the bedroom unseen?

She pushed open the wardrobe door. Now she knew where she was!

This was the grumpy Colin's room – the oldest brother's quarters, and not one of the bedrooms that she'd been allocated so far. He and his wife – well, in theory at least – shared this room. When they weren't cavorting with other people in the billiards room or the hay loft.

Thankfully, the room was empty.

The housemaids hadn't yet gotten here to clean, and it was a mess. The bed was tangled, a hip flask lay on the floor, a sherry glass was on the side table. Colin's wife Janet had also been busy in the dressing room – trying on different blouses, it seemed, from the eight or so that were scattered around.

An empty plate with a smear of sauce rested on the Persian carpet by the fireplace. Next to it, Mary saw in surprise, one of the hounds was snoozing. When it saw her emerge from the wardrobe, it lifted its head and thumped its tail briefly, clearly untroubled by this surprising apparition.

She didn't waste any more time – and now was not the moment to search for any secrets. She was already going to be unforgivably late for her tutoring appointment. Having been early, she hadn't thought she'd get stuck in a wardrobe and then have to extricate herself via a secret passage.

She hurried along the corridor, noticing that something gray and filigree was dangling in front of her. Plucking at it as she rushed around the corner, she saw a spider web was stuck to her cap.

Shuddering as she removed it, Mary hoped that the spider had remained behind and wasn't perched on the back of her head.

She didn't have time to check. It was already five past eleven, according to the grandfather clock.

This was the corridor where Master Ferdinand had his study room. His bedroom was the second-last door on the left, and the study room was all the way at the end. Preparing an apology for her tardiness, she hurried up to the door, which was slightly ajar, and pushed it open, readying herself for a hasty entrance.

She felt something move and shift at the top of the door.

And then, a soft parcel landed on her head, and the world exploded in a white, blinding cloud.

CHAPTER NINETEEN

It was flour! What felt like a ton of flour had just fallen on Mary's head, and now she was covered in it! Flour was everywhere. On her cap, on her shoulders, all over her white apron and navy blue uniform, on her shoes. It was in the air and in her eyes, and she sneezed. This caused a large wad of flour to fall off the top of her head and onto the floor, along with a large, irritated-looking spider that scuttled off toward the window, leaving a trail of flour behind him as he went.

As the flour dust cleared from the air, Mary became aware of hysterical laughter, emanating from the young, long legged man who was sitting at the desk with his feet up on it.

"Oh, that was the funniest thing I ever saw! You walked right into that, didn't you? You look like a ghost! Help, my study is haunted!" He could barely get out the words, he was spluttering so much with laughter. "The way you sneezed! Oh, that was simply classic!"

"Master Ferdinand! You – you set that trap for me?" she asked him incredulously.

They hadn't even been introduced! She'd planned to do that as soon as she walked in, but the flour bomb had derailed her plans. Now he was laughing so much he was almost falling off his chair.

The chair was an antique one, set at a desk with ornate, carved legs on the far side of the room. The flour hadn't reached here. The rug was clean and the floor was shiny and his books, some on the desk and some on the floor, looked untouched by the destruction.

"Well, I set it for whoever walked in. I knew it would be some hapless maid!"

The scorn in his voice surprised her. This young man did not have respect for anyone he considered an inferior. His tone made that abundantly clear.

And it was filling her with suspicion.

Mary had assumed him to be innocent, a sweet teenaged boy with nothing more to worry about than his studies. But here he was, pranking her in a thoroughly mean way and laughing about it to her face. One thing was obvious: he wasn't in any fear of punishment. He'd obviously decided he could do what he liked to the staff without consequences.

Now, that raised some very serious questions in her mind.

What had he done to Sarah-Jane after she'd supervised his lessons yesterday? Had they argued? Was the murder his form of retribution because she'd said she'd report his atrocious behavior? Or had his evil pranking escalated, and he'd killed her just because he could?

Maybe Ferdinand saw something in Mary's eyes, because his laughter stopped abruptly.

"Look, it was just a joke," he said. "I'll get back to my books now."

Retribution or not, Mary decided that part of studying was to learn about the consequences your actions had. Even if he'd murdered Sarah-Jane because she'd been mad at him – well, Mary wasn't going to shy away from doing what needed to be done.

"You won't get back to your books," she said.

"But I need to study!" His voice was defensive.

"That was before you caused rather an unfortunate mess in this room," Mary said firmly.

"You caused it!"

"There's flour all over the study floor. And that flour needs to be cleaned up. So we have a choice." Folding her arms, she tried to assume the selfsame tone that she remembered her mother using, on the odd occasions when she'd been mad at Mary. Her mother had managed to get a very threatening edge into her voice that had made Mary backtrack, and do what she was told, without any further resistance.

She hoped that she was channeling her mum now as she spoke. At any rate, Ferdinand was looking nervous. He took his feet off the desk and placed them on the floor.

"What choice?" he asked.

"Either we clean up the flour now, or else, we go straight to Lady Middlefield and we explain the situation to her together," Mary said, sweetly. She had a feeling that escalating the situation straight to the grand dame herself might produce the desired response.

And she was right. Ferdinand paled. She guessed that he might have had a defense prepared if she'd threatened to tell his parents – but this was a step too far up the ladder.

"Not Granny!" he said, confirming her hunch.

"Yes, Granny," she said. "We're taking this straight to the top. I happen to know she's still down at breakfast, and that's just a short walk away."

"You wouldn't do that!" he tried.

"How do you know what I would and wouldn't do?" Mary countered. "You don't know me at all. I doubt you even know my name."

There was a silence. He was fidgeting now.

"Well, what is your name?"

"My name's Mary Adams. That's not the only question you should have. The other question you should be asking is – where's the broom cupboard? I'm guessing you're not familiar with its location."

"I don't usually clean up after myself," he admitted.

"That's as important as studying," Mary said firmly. "You go down the corridor. Turn left and then right. It's the first door on the right. Bring back a bucket, a broom, and a dustpan. In the meantime, I'll take the rug outside and shake it."

There was a French door at the far end of the study, which led straight onto the gardens. She'd be able to get the rug flour-free out there and also brush the rest of the flour off her uniform.

And while she did that, she was going to think about her strategy for questioning Ferdinand.

He seemed too shocked at being told what to do by a housemaid to come up with any further argument. He walked to the door, unable to avoid stepping in the flour as he headed out. Seeing that he was leaving white footprints behind him, he started doing a frantic dance in the corridor, tapping his feet together to try to get the flour off his soles, looking so comical that now it was Mary's turn to suppress a snort of laughter.

When he'd left, she rolled up the edges of the rug, then hefted it to the French door, and outside, lifting it up and shaking it off. The rug was heavy and difficult to handle and she couldn't help thinking that this was not what she'd expected herself to be doing right now.

At any rate, the flour and the rug were both very dry, and luckily, so was the weather, so the flour didn't turn into a sticky mess. After some vigorous shaking and brushing, it was as good as new, and so was Mary's uniform.

She returned to the room to find Ferdinand already busy with the broom.

Having clearly inherited the family trait of inexpertise she'd already noticed, he was sweeping enthusiastically, but not well. Helping him as best she could, tidying up the edges of the flour spill with her dustpan and brush, the mess was soon swept up and they deposited it outside, where Mary thought it looked a little like a fresh snowfall on the green grass.

Then they both returned inside.

"Now, your studies?" she asked.

"My studies?" He looked alarmed, as if he'd expended enough effort already for the morning.

"What are you supposed to be learning this morning?" Mary decided it was now time to guide the conversation around to where she needed it to be. After all, she hadn't thought this innocent young man could be a suspect, but he'd quickly changed her mind about that.

She needed to sneakily find out what the relationship had been between him and Sarah-Jane, and what had played out in this study.

"Tell me where you finished up yesterday," she said. "Who was supervising you then?"

To her surprise, his face fell. "Sarah-Jane," he told her. "And she died last night, they said there was some kind of an accident, she slipped and fell and knocked her head."

"Is that what you heard?" Mary asked.

"Yes. And I must say, I'm rather sad about it." Giving his books an unenthusiastic glance, he lowered himself down into the chair with a sigh.

"Don't you think she's 'some hapless maid'?" Mary asked, feeding his earlier words back to him.

His fidgeting looked deeply uncomfortable now.

"Maybe I shouldn't have said that," he admitted. "It was – well, I guess after hearing that news, I was a bit out of sorts."

"Do you really think some people are inferior to others because of the job they do?" she pressured him.

"My father does!" There was audible contempt in his voice now.

"Did you set out to behave the same way he does?"

"I never want to behave like him!" He stared at her angrily. "Look, this was a practical joke. Everyone knows I'm a prankster. That's just who I am. I can't change my behavior. And I never want to be like my father!"

It was clearly obvious that he was heading the exact same way, but since he couldn't see it for himself, she saw no point in trying to keep telling him. But now, she wanted to know what his relationship with Sarah-Jane had been.

"You knew Sarah-Jane? Had she supervised you before?"

He nodded, swinging back in his chair, his legs crossed and his arms laced behind his head. "Yes. She was the regular stand-in for my tutor when he couldn't get here. She'd done some student teaching in the past, she told me. Not that she talked about her past much," he said thoughtfully.

"And what did you think of Sarah-Jane?" This was a key question, and she paid close attention to the answer.

"She was a good person. I liked her. She was fun. She laughed about things. We both laughed together. And she was like you, she had – well, a forceful personality. I kind of enjoyed that. Too many people in this place just tiptoe around me," he said, irritably.

She had a forceful personality. That was the first person who'd ever told her such a thing. She felt very relieved she'd been able to summon up her mother's strict demeanor at the exact moment when it was needed.

"Did you argue with her at all yesterday?"

"No, I didn't. I did notice that she was looking a bit – well, a bit distracted. I asked her if anything was wrong, but she said no. She said she'd met someone who'd made her wonder if she should have done things differently."

"Is that so?" Mary's curiosity was thoroughly aroused now. Yesterday, Sarah-Jane had tutored Ferdinand at exactly the same time of day, before luncheon. And by that time, something had already happened to make her thoughtful and distracted, and not like her usual sunny self?

Was this something different from the crisis she'd told Mary about?

Or had this situation escalated later in the day, and had this been the reason for her panicked buzzing to Mary, so late at night?

How she wished she knew more. But Ferdinand clearly didn't have any more information, and she'd been very lucky to get what she had.

"So, what lesson are you busy with?" she asked.

"English and mathematics," he replied. "I hate them both, but we did mathematics yesterday and I think I hate it more."

"Let's focus on English today, then," she said, relieved that this was probably more within her area of expertise than mathematics was.

But, as she took the study book and turned to the questions page, ready to test him on his knowledge, a troubling thought occurred to her.

There *was* somebody who knew about Sarah-Jane's past. Someone who was staying at Middlefield Manor and who had been in the manor at the time of the murder.

Gilbert might know more about this – a lot more. But how could she question him about Sarah-Jane? She had the feeling that if she did, it would ruin the friendship - or whatever it was turning into – between them.

With a sinking of her heart, as she listened to Ferdinand's rather clumsy analysis of the Rime of the Ancient Mariner, Mary knew that there was no choice. Like it or not, Gilbert MacLeod was a suspect, and she'd need to treat him that way.

CHAPTER TWENTY

The luncheon gong had sounded long before Mary allowed Ferdinand to leave his study. If he was going to delay things by setting flour traps, she reasoned, then she was going to make up the time at the end of the session, even if it cut into lunch. That was the price you paid for pranking people.

Thanking her – which she was surprised about – Ferdinand rushed off to lunch, and Mary headed down to the staff pantry for her break. She needed to bounce some ideas off Hannah.

The staff pantry was a hive of activity. Servants, all hungry after a long morning's work, were thronging into the small, cramped space and squashing up along the benches once they'd loaded their plates with food.

There was Hannah, to her relief. And even better, there was just enough space at the end of the bench for her to squeeze in.

Conversation was still muted, but as she quickly filled her plate, Mary could hear that it was no longer focused on the murder. People were talking about other things. The possibility of an upcoming warm spell that had been announced on the BBC radio station earlier in the morning. The likelihood of the local spring fair being held in their village this year instead of the village over the hill, the possibility that a few single young horse grooms would be joining the staff if the family expanded their stables.

She listened to the conversation with one ear while piling her plate with breakfast leftovers. That was what the servants got for lunch. It made sense, in a non wasteful way, and she personally loved breakfast for lunch. At least she'd get the chance to taste one of those fishcakes. Even though, after what had happened this morning, she couldn't bring herself to eat any of the beans.

With two sausages, a fishcake, and a big cheese scone on her plate, she squashed in next to Hannah.

First things first. She cut a big slice of the fishcake and devoured it. After all, as her mum had always used to say, nobody could think their best on an empty stomach.

Hannah was piling beans on top of a piece of ham, so when they'd both finished their mouthfuls, Mary decided it was time for the important conversation to start.

"Any more gossip?" she whispered.

"Yes. There is actually something," Hannah whispered back.

"What is it?" Anything would be good now. Anything other than confronting Gilbert.

"When I was talking to Dickens earlier, there was something that I forgot to mention to you," she said.

"And what's that?"

"Dickens said he wasn't sure how the family had been able to afford a whole extra barn of horses, including one of the champion hunters in the county. He said that until a few years ago, the estate was struggling."

"And then? What happened?"

"He doesn't know. He guesses that maybe somebody died and left them some money. Or, at any rate, something happened."

"That sounds – well, interesting," Mary said.

"Dickens said that Colin was spending a lot of time in the old store room down the hill, during the later part of the war. But he doesn't know why."

"The old store room?" At that nugget of information, Mary's ears pricked up.

This sounded like an important new angle for them to investigate. And better still, it was an angle that didn't involve Gilbert MacLeod. Perhaps the family were up to something that involved that old store room, although she couldn't think what it could be.

But the chest in Lady Middlefield's room had yielded up a secret she hadn't expected, and maybe this storeroom down the hill would do the same.

"Are we going to go and investigate it?" she asked.

Hannah's eyes widened. "I hadn't considered that possibility," she admitted. "But I suppose that we have to."

"After lunch would be a good time," Mary said. "Almost all the guests have gone home now." Apart from Gilbert, and hopefully, with the guests now departed, he could have his conversation with Colin at last. That would mean both he and Colin would be occupied. And everyone else, after so much time socializing, and a late dinner last night, might be enjoying a well earned nap.

"There's another rainstorm supposed to be coming in the late afternoon," Hannah said. "I heard the housekeeper and butler discussing the weather earlier. So…" She lowered her voice still further. "This might be the only chance we have."

"We need to take it," Mary agreed. "But we need to be very careful. Remember that if Sarah-Jane found this out, she died because of it. We should probably go down there separately. If we go together, somebody might notice."

"Yes, I agree. I think one of us needs to sneak down through the stables. If you go out the back of that building, there's a path going that way."

"And the other one of us could take the route via the summerhouse. It's not in use now, and if you get past there, then it will block the view from the manor," Mary said, holding the image of the estate's layout in her mind as best she could.

"I'll go past the summerhouse with some towels," Hannah said.

"And I'll go past the stables," Mary resolved.

Their plan was set, and they decided on the time of two p.m.

Officially, Hannah was supposed to be cleaning the ballroom at that time.

"I guess they won't notice if I'm a half hour late," she said. "I'm the only one cleaning it, and there's nobody going to be using it this afternoon."

Mary consulted her list.

"I should be preparing the parlor for the guests' tea – but that was yesterday's list, and the guests have all left today. Well, there's only Gilbert left. I think I can risk doing it later than usual."

Their window of opportunity was presenting itself. Now, they just had to take advantage of it.

With resolve filling her, Mary got up and went over to the sideboard, stealing the second-last Scotch egg. They looked delicious, and she needed to make sure she was fortified for whatever the afternoon might bring.

Even though this was an adventure, she couldn't let herself forget that at any moment, it could turn deadly.

She waited for half an hour before leaving the kitchens, making good use of the time by helping to clean the staff lunch plates away, and mopping the floor yet again. It was astonishing how often that floor needed mopping to stay sparkling clean with so many people passing through.

Glancing at the clock, she felt more and more nervous and expectant as the time approached.

Finally, half an hour had passed. Choosing her moment carefully, and making sure that everyone's attention was elsewhere, Mary sneaked out of the scullery door and took a roundabout route down to the stables, passing behind the privet maze and giving the rose garden a very wide berth. After all, Lady Middlefield's bedroom had a view of it, and she didn't want anyone, especially the sharp-eyed lady, to see her.

She reached the stable barn and walked inside, breathing in the scent of fresh straw, listening to the rustling and munching sounds as the horses moved within their stables. The grooms were at work, letting some horses out to the field, with big waterproof canvas blankets draped over them. And bringing other horses in – their legs, manes and blankets encrusted with mud.

That would all need to be cleaned off, Hannah saw, as she shrank back into the saddlery room as a groom passed by, leading two horses.

Expanding the stables was clearly a lot more work, and it would take a lot more people. It wasn't just the cost of buying the hunters, it was the ongoing cost of their hay, their feed, their equipment, and the grooms looking after them, who all had to be paid a salary.

So, what had happened, exactly, to make all of this possible? And was the answer hidden away in the store room, whose roof she could now see from the barn's south door?

She checked left and right before hurrying out of the barn, wrapping her arms around her to shield against the worsening wind. The sky was darkening, and a threatening bank of cloud was looming from the north.

Rushing up to the store room, Mary assessed the situation.

The room, built of solid stone blocks, with big wooden barn doors, seemed impenetrable. The doors were closed tight. She pulled experimentally at one and then the other as hard as she could. No. They didn't pull open. How about pushing? It didn't seem as likely, but she gave it a try.

Still nothing. They wouldn't budge, and weren't even moving. And they were eight feet high, and looked very solid. What if they were locked, and they couldn't get in at all?

Worse still, out here on the hillside, it was an exposed place. Anyone could see her here, and then what would happen?

Maybe there was another way in, other than tugging ineffectually at the doors?

Wondering where Hannah was, and hoping nothing had gone wrong, Mary left the exposed front wall of the building, and sneaked around the side.

This was better. Looking up at the white-painted wall, she saw a high, narrow pair of windows.

If she could get up there somehow, she could peek inside. But how?

At that moment, over the whistle of the wind, she heard the swift patter of footsteps.

Hannah rushed up to the building just as Mary peeked around the side and beckoned her there.

"The doors won't budge," she whispered. "But there are two windows."

Hannah followed her around the side. Mary's skirts blew against her ankles, and the wind ruffled her hair under the white lacy cap as they both stared up at the windows.

"They're rather high," Hannah said.

"They are." Again, Mary wished for a ladder. But bringing a ladder down here would attract far too much attention.

"One of us could stand on the other's shoulders!" Finally, inspiration struck.

"Who will be underneath?" Hannah asked. They glanced at each other.

Mary was taller than Hannah, and she had strong shoulders. Much as she wanted to be the one to grab the window frame and peek inside, she knew that she had a better chance of holding Hannah steady, than the other way around.

"I'll hold you," she said.

It was an awkward and slippery business. Luckily, Mary had the presence of mind to take off her white apron and her cap before they started, because otherwise they would both have been smeared with mud.

As it was, by the time she'd managed to bend down, braced against the wall, and have Hannah scramble onto her back, and then manage to get one of her feet onto her shoulder, and then straighten up really slowly, so that Hannah didn't slip, she had several muddy streaks on her hands and neck.

But she'd done it. Hannah was on her shoulders, with her feet planted squarely on each side of Mary's neck, and that meant Hannah was now high up enough to see what was inside those windows.

Trembling with the effort of holding her, Mary kept her feet steady and stared at the wall in front of her nose.

"Well, what's there?"

"I'm looking," came the whispered words from above, also quivering with strain.

"And? What can you see?"

"Well, this is the strange thing!" Hannah was breathing hard. Mary could feel her feet shifting as her weight moved as she stared around.

"What's strange?"

"I'm looking and looking. And there's nothing there at all. The place is totally empty!"

"What?" Mary asked incredulously. "Are you sure?"

"I'm looking everywhere! There's nothing. It's a big open space, and there's nothing inside whatsoever. The floor looks swept clean. And I can see some scrape marks on one side – as if something was there, but it isn't there anymore."

"That's so strange!"

"I'd look further," Hannah's voice was strangled. "But I'd only be trying to make something appear in my imagination. And also, I didn't mention this before now, but I'm rather scared of heights!"

"Alright then." As steadily as possible, Mary bent her knees, now feeling Hannah's legs quivering. Finally, when her own legs were about to give in, Hannah was able to half-slide, half-scramble down. She landed on the grass with a thump, and although Mary did her best to grab her, she wasn't quite fast enough to stop Hannah from landing on her backside.

They stared at each other in puzzlement.

Totally empty? It had to mean something. Why would an empty storeroom be so tightly closed? And Hannah had said the floor had looked clean, so it had been in use, but wasn't now.

She didn't know what it meant.

Huddled behind the barn, in the worsening wind, they brushed off the grass stains and cleaned up their shoes, and the smears of mud on Mary's hands and neck, evidence of the exploration that had got them precisely nowhere. If only there had been something in that room to help them understand why Sarah-Jane had been murdered.

But whatever they were searching for, Mary guessed it wasn't there.

"Am I clean enough to go back to work?" she asked.

"Yes. You're very clean." Lifting her hand, Hannah wiped away the last trace of mud from Mary's chin.

“And let me check your skirt?”

Hannah turned around, and Mary brushed the final specks of mud and grass away before she put her apron back on. Now, they looked respectable again – and it was time for them to hurry back to work.

She wasn’t going to go directly back to work, though. There was one place she needed to be first.

With every other avenue exhausted, it was time for her to explore the last resort that she’d really hoped she wouldn’t have to.

CHAPTER TWENTY ONE

Heading back inside the manor via a discreet side door, Mary was startled to hear the words, "Hey, Mary. Hey there!"

Her name was being called, in a soft, urgent hiss.

She spun around, heart quickening, to see Barry. Approaching from the corridor, his gaze was fixed on her.

"Listen, I wanted to check with you – after our… our episode earlier. I wanted to make absolutely sure you know it's just a bit of – of cousinly competitiveness, and that it's quite important not to tell anybody?"

"You asked me that earlier," Mary pointed out.

"I know. But you, well – you didn't give a totally clear answer. What I mean is, I'd like to check with you again. I'm keen to get your word that you definitely won't tell anyone."

"I'm not prepared to give you my word on that," Mary said.

She couldn't lie. She was planning on telling someone. At the very least, she was going to have to warn poor Martin not to eat any more beans, or preferably anything at all, brought to him by his ever so loving cousin.

"I'd like to have a proper conversation with you about this," Barry pleaded. "I know you said you don't like jewels, and I respect that decision. But how do you feel about a magnificent golden necklace? No jewels! Not a ruby or emerald in sight. Just good old solid gold!"

"No," Mary said, gently but firmly. "Sir, I can't keep discussing this. I'm very busy."

That wasn't entirely true. She'd been 'busy' doing her own investigating in the past half hour, and not the duties she was being paid to do.

"I know, I can see how hard you work. I'd really like to offer you something –"

This had gone too far. In Barry's now anguished face, Mary could see the truth of it. He really wanted to offer her something – money maybe, or jewelry, to buy her silence. And it seemed that was a family trait, because they'd also done it to the inspector.

"I cannot continue this conversation now," she said, firmly. It seemed appallingly rude to simply turn her back and walk away from a member of the household, but he was leaving her no choice.

"Later then?" His pleading words followed her, but Mary didn't look back.

Now, with Barry on the alert, she couldn't go straight to Gilbert MacLeod's room. Having Barry follow her there could be extremely awkward for everyone.

So instead, she turned in the direction of the billiards room, then took the corridor leading up to an attic room where three of the butlers stayed, and then she doubled back, coming out of a door further along.

No sign of Barry. That was a relief. She fervently hoped that he'd give up on this. Really, what he should do was go and apologize to his cousin and come clean about what he'd been doing.

Putting the thoughts of Barry out of her mind, Mary tried to come up with a plan as she approached Gilbert's room.

Would he be inside here? Or would he still be in conversation with Colin, trying to finalize the arrangement with those seeds?

She tapped on the door, feeling nerves surge inside her. It felt like a lot had happened recently between her and Gilbert. They'd gone from being mere acquaintances, to having had much more to do with each other. They'd even had – well, you couldn't call it an argument, but it had been a spirited discussion. He'd wanted to protect her and stop her from putting herself in danger. She hadn't wanted to be protected and hadn't cared about the danger.

It was clear that he wasn't in his room.

She could go in, on the pretext of tidying, and take a look around. After all, from what Ferdinand had said, it may have been the encounter with Gilbert that had left Sarah-Jane feeling thoughtful and troubled.

Pushing open the door, Mary stepped inside, feeling guilty and torn about doing this at all. It was wrong to snoop. But then again, a lot of things that had happened recently were wrong, and a lot of people in this manor had surprised her so far.

It wouldn't be snooping, she decided, if she simply tidied the room and, in doing so, took a look at what was there. She couldn't bring herself to open his suitcase or his drawers and rifle through his possessions. That would be utterly impossible.

But she could walk over to the bed and move this cup, glancing down as she did so.

There was nothing on the antique nightstand by the bed except a neatly folded handkerchief. She noted that Gilbert kept his room tidy, far tidier than the mess the Middlefield men seemed to strew in their wake.

What about here, on the desk? She could move the small vase of pine needles that had been placed there as a welcoming touch, and clean around it.

And when she did that, she saw the item that was behind it.

Why was this on the desk at all? She could think of only one reason, which was that he must have recently been looking at it.

It was a photo album, and it was open at the first page. Staring down in consternation, Mary realized this put everything in a different light. Everything.

She'd promised herself that she wouldn't snoop, but it was beyond her self control not to turn the page, and look at the photos on the next page. And then, the one after that.

It was the strangest sequence of photos she'd ever seen. And it told a story that explained a lot.

The first photos were of two boys standing in front of a humble little cottage.

The next photo was similar, only it was the boys with their parents. Frowning, Mary took in the size of this tiny cottage, the glimpse of frilly curtains in the window, the proud expressions on the parents' faces. The mother had one hand on each of the boys' shoulders; the father was holding a small, wire-haired mongrel on a leash.

On the next page was a photo clearly taken at school, of a boy with dark hair, a cheeky expression and an impish smile, and those trademark freckles on his face.

Without a doubt, it was Gilbert. There was another photo of him cuddling that same dog.

The next page of photographs showed some kind of a factory. It was small and humble-looking, and the father was standing in front of it, beaming proudly. Then, the next one showed furniture – really well designed and attractive chairs and tables, that looked solid and quality and made with superb workmanship. Another photo of the father, smiling – this time in front of a bigger house.

The next page showed photos of two new factories, both larger, and a range of furniture – chairs, tables, headboards, bed frames, chests of drawers, wardrobes, and some ranges of living room furniture, too. There were cots and desks and bookshelves and benches, bar tables and bar stools, an interior of a fully decked out restaurant, another of a dining hall on a cruise ship.

The furniture was not the type she saw in the stately homes, but it was the type that any ordinary family would be proud to own. Quality, beautifully made, but she guessed it was also affordable to many, rather than being priced to suit the pockets of only a few.

With a sense of unreality, Mary realized that she was following the creation of an empire – a humble little manufacturing business that had made it big and then huge, bringing financial success that must have been beyond the founders' wildest dreams.

And the founders were Gilbert's parents!

Not upper class born and bred, but working class who'd come up with a great business concept, at the right time.

That was why Gilbert had known Sarah-Jane. They had attended the same school because they had been from the same local village and in the same circumstances.

But Gilbert had never mentioned this, and now, Mary was wondering why.

Was he ashamed of his background?

Was this a secret he would do anything to hide – even going as far as murder?

As those dark thoughts were crowding her mind, she heard rapid footsteps approach, and her heart accelerated.

CHAPTER TWENTY TWO

Fingers fumbling with haste, Mary turned the album page back to the first one when she'd found it, and stepped away. Picking up the dirty cup, she turned to the bedroom door with what she hoped was a professional expression.

But as Gilbert walked through the doorway, and saw her there, his gaze went immediately, and guiltily, to that photo album. She noticed it clearly and without a doubt.

"Good afternoon," she said politely, even though a cold feeling had settled inside her. No wonder he'd pleaded with her not to investigate the case. It was because he'd been worried about this – exactly this – happening.

There was no room for lies. Not anymore.

"While I was tidying the table, I happened to notice that album," Mary said, standing as straight and tall as she could while she spoke, as if her posture might help her with the courage it was taking to speak these words.

Gilbert flinched visibly.

"The album. Yes, of course – the album," he said. "I meant to put it away before anyone could see it. I – well, I guess I owe you an explanation about it. And an apology for not telling you sooner."

"I had a look through the photos," Mary admitted. "You weren't always wealthy, were you? That's how you and your family knew Sarah-Jane?"

It was chilling to think that she was having this conversation with a man who might well have killed to keep his secrets. Betrayal felt like an acid, burning at her insides.

Gilbert stepped forward. He grimaced angrily. Never before had Mary seen him look angry. It was a new expression for him. There was a lot she was learning about Gilbert MacLeod right now.

"It's the real reason I came here," he admitted.

"What is?" she asked, not understanding him at all. But she also was not allowing herself to hope that his reason would make sense, either. There might be a logical explanation for all of this, but she couldn't think of one.

It seemed impossible to imagine this likeable, pleasant-faced man, who'd always been so kind to her, as a killer – and yet, he had secrets of a depth and scale she'd never imagined.

"Look, let me go back in time and explain things to you," he offered.

Turning, he closed the door. That action, though simple, gave Mary a deep chill. Now, she was alone in the room with him. It might be that he didn't want anyone to overhear what he was going to say – but it might also be that he was planning on killing again.

Gilbert? Could he really be the murderer? Even with the door now firmly closed, she was having difficulty thinking of him this way. She had to remind herself that Sarah-Jane had also believed she was working with people she trusted. And look what had happened to her.

"Explain, then," she said. She didn't want to give away how uneasy she now felt, but even she could hear the wobble in her voice.

"Well." Gilbert walked over to the desk. He sat down at the mahogany chair and gestured to the seat of the blue-upholstered armchair for Mary to do the same. Not that she wanted to sit down right now, but she was willing to hear him out. If only because it would give her the evidence she needed.

"He is not what he seems."

That warning applied to nobody more accurately than Gilbert MacLeod.

"You see," he began, in an unsteady voice, "we were just ordinary people. My parents, my brother Robert, myself, and our dog, Holly. We grew up in a little village near Glasgow. But my dad – he always loved making things with his hands, and he had this idea of a quality, affordable furniture range that he could create blueprints for and make in bulk, but then personalize with painting, varnishing and so on."

"I understand that?" Mary's hands were tightly clenched as she listened. There wasn't a sound coming from outside the bedroom. Nobody else was nearby.

"Anyway, it was a huge success. I remember, as a little child, I'd toddle around the factory and I could get from one side to the other in no time. Then it expanded, and they bought up new premises, and soon, it covered an entire large building. Then two buildings. Then, by the time I was a teenager, it took me a few minutes to walk from one end of the operation to the other. There were a few different buildings, a lumber yard, a delivery section – we sent furniture by road, and by train and even by ship."

“So that was the reason for your wealth?” Mary asked.

Gilbert nodded. “Yes. It all happened over the space of about ten or twelve years. We ended up buying a big estate – not that my parents really wanted it, but the owner fell on hard times and approached us, and we ended up doing the deal, and then just like that, we became part of the gentry."

Now, there was an uneasy look in his eyes, and Mary had the feeling this was where his story was going to take a darker turn.

"That's a lovely success story." There was a cynical note in her voice, and Gilbert's head turned sharply as he picked it up. "But where does the need to hide the photo album come into it?"

“It was my mother,” he said.

He wasn’t looking at her. He was staring at the floor.

“Your mother, how?”

“It’s difficult to say this. It sounds – well, embarrassing,” he admitted. He glanced at her and she was surprised to see a trace of the liveliness she was used to seeing, in his face once more. “My mother quickly realized that a lot of the upper classes have a frankly terrible attitude toward poorer people.”

“Yes,” Mary said, understanding this point, even though she didn’t yet see where his argument was going. “Many of them are very snobbish, I’m afraid to say.”

“To make it worse, we were welcomed in a very friendly way by the other families in the area, who owned big estates,” Gilbert said. “They didn’t know our poor background, and before my parents could explain, my mother had already become aware that – well, some of the nicer families might not have minded, but some of the less nice ones would look at us differently. By then, we'd already overheard those people's opinions on the working classes, so it would be seen as if we'd intentionally misled them."

That wasn’t what Mary had expected to hear at all. She could see that it would be an intensely embarrassing situation if such a fact came to light too late. But she was still wary of what the MacLeod family, and Gilbert, in particular, might have done to protect this secret.

“My mother in particular had made some good friends, after years of being quite friendless, and supporting my dad in the factory, and raising us. So she made us promise that we would keep this background a secret, just so that it didn’t jeopardize something that was very important to her. And my dad and I, who didn’t care as much, agreed.”

Gilbert sighed, burying his head briefly in his hands and tugging at his hair before raising it again. "It wouldn't have affected our main business, because our furniture isn't sold through word of mouth or to anyone in the upper class echelon. It's just put in stores and people buy it. But by then we'd also started a few other ventures – the seeds, the forestry, and my mum has started doing some design of interiors for these stately homes. She's got quite a knack for it. I have a folder of examples in the car, and I spread the word wherever I go."

So, business interests, too, had ended up being at stake?

She understood everything so far. But Mary dreaded that the turning point of this conversation still lay ahead.

"How does this all relate to Sarah-Jane?" she asked in a small voice.

"I came to make Sarah-Jane a job offer. Again," he said.

Mary certainly had not expected that.

"A job offer?" she asked incredulously.

"Yes," Gilbert said. "Last time I was here, which was a quick meeting to introduce myself and the seeds, I was astounded to see her, and so was she to see me. We had a good talk, and I updated her on everything that had happened. She agreed not to say anything but – you know, driving away, I thought maybe there was an opportunity for her. Being in her late thirties, perhaps she was looking for a career that was less hard work and where she could grow and progress."

"Go on?" Mary said.

"I discussed it with my parents and they agreed. She was such a good carer to us at the school, and such a nice person, who'd been so well respected in our village. And at one of the factories, there was a very good job with a generous salary, that was available for somebody to do the accounts and keep the books. She's always had a head for figures – I remember that from my schooldays. So I came back this time to offer her the job."

Mary felt absolutely stunned.

She could not have been more wrong about the entire situation.

This had been a job offer? Not threatening Sarah-Jane with consequences if she said a word about the family's background – which she'd already agreed not to talk about. But something positive – a new job. It made Mary feel terrible that she'd suspected Gilbert of being a killer, and it also made her feel strangely sad that Sarah-Jane had never been able to take up what sounded like a wonderful offer.

"She refused it, of course," Gilbert said, and Mary's eyes flew wider.

"Refused it?"

"Yes."

"But why? Why would she refuse an offer like that?"

Gilbert shrugged. "She said she's always made her own way in life, and this felt like charity, and that the Middlefield family has been very good to her."

Mary was now left totally breathless.

The reason for Gilbert's visit, the reason for Sarah-Jane's thoughtfulness after her conversation with him, which Ferdinand had noticed when she had tutored him – they were for a different reason entirely, and nothing to do with the fact that Gilbert had threatened her. Quite the opposite. He'd offered her a great opportunity, which she'd chosen not to accept.

"The family has been good to her," Mary echoed, just to fill the silence that had descended.

"That's right," Gilbert said.

A family that had been good to her – and yet, she'd been killed? It didn't make sense at all. Gilbert had been her final suspect, the last person that she'd thought could have a motive. Now, Sarah-Jane's own words to him were ruling out any other direction she might have had.

Unless, perhaps, she'd said something more?

"What exactly did she tell you about the family?" she said in a low voice, remembering that Sarah-Jane, too, had been wary of being overheard.

When she'd talked to Gilbert, she had clearly felt that she was in a safe place where she was looked after. That had been in the morning. But by the time night had fallen, she'd been frightened, paranoid, and thoroughly flustered.

So, now at least she knew that something must have happened in between those two times.

Maybe Gilbert, unknowingly, had picked up some information that might explain this.

"What did she tell me about the family?" he repeated thoughtfully. "I was – well, I was a bit shocked that she'd refused my offer so abruptly. I mean, it was almost as if she'd been offended by it. I was feeling insensitive, like I'd come along offering her a kind of charity that she had no interest in accepting. It was very embarrassing. I felt like I was misusing my position as a wealthier person when all I'd intended was to help her and offer her something I thought she'd like."

Gilbert seemed genuinely distressed by what had played out. He was not faking this. An offer had been made in a good spirit, and now he was chastising himself for having extended that helping hand.

He might have been too disconcerted by Sarah-Jane's refusal to remember anything at all, Mary thought sadly.

But then, his face lit up. "Actually, she did give me some information that I thought was interesting – and rather strange. In fact, I didn't understand how it could be true."

CHAPTER TWENTY THREE

"What information was this?" Mary asked Gilbert. She felt breathless as she waited for his reply. This was pivotal to the investigation. Something 'rather strange' might crack this strange mystery all the way open.

It wasn't going to be as easy as she thought to get the information, though, because now he was backtracking.

"Listen, Mary, I – well, I don't think I should tell you." He folded his arms, and a worried frown creased his face.

"Why not?"

"Because it could prove too risky for you. I'm worried about you. What if – what if I tell you, and the same thing happens to you?"

Information from Sarah-Jane herself? This could prove critical to finding the killer. What could she do to persuade Gilbert to tell her? Thinking about how she could proceed, Mary noticed again how quiet the room was.

Or was it? Was that a footfall she could hear outside?

Remembering how scared Sarah-Jane had been about people listening, Mary stood up. She couldn't risk that somebody was spying on them here.

"Can you wait a minute?" she asked Gilbert.

She strode over to the door, ready to fling it open. But, as she reached the door, she heard the distinctive sound of running footsteps, retreating fast.

"Wait!" Shouting out the word, Mary flung open the door. Somebody had been listening. Her instinct had been correct.

But it was too late. The running person had disappeared.

Were they out of sight, whoever they were? Those footsteps had darted to the left. Turning left, Mary ran at full speed down the corridor, past one more closed bedroom door, and then skidded around the bend in the passage.

It stretched ahead – with a branch to the left and the right. Whoever was listening at the door could have gone in any one of the three directions. She couldn't tell which way it had been, and there were no further footsteps to be heard.

She headed back to the bedroom to find Gilbert standing in the doorway, staring frantically to the left and the right.

"What on earth happened there?" he asked.

"Someone was listening at the door," Mary told him, hearing the tension in her own voice.

"Listening at the – good heavens!" Gilbert blinked rapidly. "This must be to do with the murder, then?"

"I'm sure it was." The killer himself must have been outside. If only she'd been faster. She'd missed him by a hair's breadth, and she hadn't been able to pick up a thing from those desperately running footsteps, about who the runner had been.

After having looked both ways again, just in case, she closed the door once more. Then, she walked over and checked the window. They were on the second floor, so the chances of anyone listening outside was slim, but she still wanted to make sure.

Nobody hanging onto the drainpipe, nobody crouched in the flower bed or behind the rhododendrons. And the weather was closing in fast. There was such a wind blowing now that nobody outside, down below, could hear anything.

Reassured by that, she returned to her seat. But adrenaline was fizzing inside her. She perched on the armchair, unable to relax, wanting to run to the door and wrench it open again and see if anyone was there.

"Mary, you really need to be careful," Gilbert said in a serious voice, though it was only a little above a whisper.

But Mary swung around to face him and said, in a whisper just as serious, "No. *You* need to be careful!"

"What do you mean?" Gilbert asked, looking taken aback by her words.

"Whoever this was, they were listening at your bedroom door, not mine. Whatever this secret is, it's possible you know it. It might be that Sarah-Jane knew something about it, without knowing that she knew. And that she told you in innocence."

There was a silence in the room.

They both looked at the door again.

Although Mary couldn't hear any more stealthy sounds outside, it only took one set of hastily departing footfalls to make you feel paranoid – as she had just discovered. Maybe it was overkill, but better safe than sorry. She tiptoed to the door again and peered through the keyhole.

Then, she grabbed the handle and flung it open with such a bang that Gilbert jumped.

Leaping into the corridor, she checked to see if anyone was sneaking back. But there was nobody outside. Whoever the listener had been, she didn't think they were coming back.

Closing the door firmly, she returned to the armchair and perched on it again.

"So, it seems that whatever she told you might have been important. And that you should be taking care, not me. Whoever hit Sarah-Jane – they did it so hard they left a dent in her forehead," Mary breathed. "They must have used a very solid iron bar. And a woman's head isn't any softer than a man's. They could lay in wait for you and – thwack."

Gilbert flinched again, but Mary wasn't holding back.

"This killer could hit anyone, just like that."

"I mind if they hit you, more than I mind if they hit me," he argued, showing a surprisingly stubborn side that until now had escaped her attention. But Mary was ready to take it on, and she had her argument prepared.

"They might already think I know. After all, I've been talking to you in here for a while now." Guiltily, she remembered that her preparation of the parlor was now overdue. The only redeeming factor was that she was currently talking to the last remaining guest still at the manor. Tea for one would only happen when Gilbert left his room. "If someone's watching from a distance now, they'll know how long I've been in here and that it's more than enough time for secrets to be told," she added.

"Oh, dear." He clasped his hands and twisted his fingers together. "Mary, this is terrible. I'd do whatever it took to keep you out of danger, but it now seems you might be in it already."

"It's highly likely," she acknowledged. "So, the only way out of the danger is to figure out who this killer is, and fast."

He sighed. "Well, in that case, you've persuaded me."

"Sssh!" Mary leaned forward, finger on her lips, because his voice had risen enough that she thought it could be heard from outside..

Hastily, he lowered his tone again. "I'll tell you, but – well, I'm not leaving here until this is solved. I can't drive away from this place, knowing that you might be in danger and that there's a killer on the loose. Whatever I can do to help you, I will do."

This situation was becoming more and more complicated. Middlefield Manor was now going to have a guest who refused to depart! That could be exceedingly awkward. She didn't think it would enhance Gilbert's chances of striking up a friendly relationship with Colin Middlefield, if such a thing was even possible. But she also didn't think that Gilbert cared about that.

What he cared about now was her.

That fact made her feel warm inside and oddly vulnerable in a way that she hadn't felt before in her years of living alone.

That was strange, wasn't it? She should feel safe, knowing somebody cared. But instead, it felt as if a door had been opened, and that now all her feelings might end up pouring out of it. Only at this moment was Mary acknowledging how tightly she'd kept a lot of those feelings locked up since her mum had died.

Well, there was nothing she could do about it. She couldn't exactly stop it from happening and would just have to deal with the aftermath.

The most important thing was, in this battle of wills – and wits – her argument had managed to convince him. And now Gilbert was drawing a deep breath before letting it out in an almost inaudible whisper.

"She told me that the manor house had gone through hard times, a few years ago, and that they'd ended up dismissing a few of their staff."

"Really?" Mary asked, her eyes widening. She hadn't seen any evidence of hard times in the manor house recently. It had seemed that there was plenty of everything – food, money, treasures, and even horses.

"They kept her on, because they said they really didn't want to dismiss anyone who was so loyal and who'd been with them for so long. And she told me she really valued that, especially during the war years, when things were very difficult. A lot of servants were left without jobs, you know, because so many of us were at war, so many houses ended up standing empty, or operating with only a skeleton staff."

Mary guessed that Gilbert must have fought in the war, too, but with a headshake, he explained otherwise.

"My brother and I went to enlist, but they told us that since we were on a large estate, and food production was so important, we weren't allowed to. So we stayed on the estate and grew as many crops as we possibly could. We farmed a few fallow fields, we tripled our grain production, we had bumper crops of fruit, and we also branched out into cattle. So we did what we could – and that's actually where my idea for seeds was born."

She guessed that by virtue of owning farmlands, a lot of the upper classes had not been eligible to fight on the frontlines – but at least they'd kept people's stomachs full, soldiers and civilians alike.

It was strange how quickly you forgot about such hardships, she thought. While working at the factory, there had been rationing strictly in place for all of them. Sugar had been restricted, meat was a luxury, and often during the worst times, after a hard day working with heavy machinery in the cold, she'd gone home to nothing more than a dinner of hot water and brown bread.

That had been how things were, and they'd all had to tighten their belts and keep their chins up during the tough times.

There was another memory, that she had of those times, involving Mr. Watson, the factory owner. At that moment though, there wasn't time to think about it, or to recall it in much detail.

"Your crop growing was a blessing to us," she said. "The days when we could get apples – or a nice piece of meat – those were very good days."

"I'm glad," he said. "Hard times for everybody, though. But anyway, that was the situation that Sarah-Jane told me." His voice lowered once again. "She said they'd been kind to her and she would be loyal to them in turn."

"Did she mention anyone's name in particular?" Mary asked.

"Not really," Gilbert shook his head, looking perplexed.

Frustratingly, Mary couldn't see anything important that would have been said during this conversation. It might have been that whatever dangerous fact she found out had happened later, and it wasn't related to her dialog with Gilbert at all.

"What else did she say?" she asked.

Sometimes, the right question or even the right word could jog people's memories. She'd experienced that in the past. Maybe, if Gilbert thought harder about that conversation, more details might come back to him.

He was frowning now, in a thoughtful way, as if they were doing just that.

"Well, I asked her a bit about the farming that they'd done here," Gilbert said. "I was – well, a little embarrassed by how the conversation had gone, and was looking for a topic that would help us move past that moment. And farming is something I'm interested in, you know, having been doing the same further north."

"Did she know much about that?" Mary asked.

“Well, no,” Gilbert admitted. “She didn’t know much about it at all. But she said something intriguing. She said there was an extraordinary amount of activity on the estate during that time. She didn’t know why -she thought perhaps it was a hub for some kind of logistics. Colin was very involved with it. There were people coming and going, trucks leaving at strange hours, and whatever farming it was seemed to pay dividends, because the estate seemed to get back on track, they rehired a lot of workers, and things seemed on an even keel again.”

Now, that was interesting.

Farming?

But had it really been farming, Mary wondered. Or had something else been happening on the estate?

Perhaps, after her conversation with Gilbert, Sarah-Jane had been reminded about that strangeness, and had gone to find out more.

CHAPTER TWENTY FOUR

Mary was sure that the answers to Sarah-Jane's death lay in the conversation she'd had with Gilbert and in what had happened afterward.

The problem was – how could she find out what Sarah-Jane had discovered?

She closed the door to Gilbert's bedroom, having left there after he'd told her this.

That had been done purposely.

She'd managed to hide her excitement about his words because she didn't want Gilbert to worry about her. If he worried about her, or thought she was onto something, he was going to follow her, and then it might go badly for everybody.

So she'd made sure to look puzzled, and shake her head, and whisper, "Probably just making conversation. What a pity she didn't say more."

As soon as she was out of the bedroom, Mary hurried to the parlor.

It was time to arrange the parlor for tea, but while she was doing it, she was going to think over what she'd learned. Perhaps she had enough puzzle pieces right now, and it was just a case of arranging them in an order that made sense.

She reached the parlor. First job was to stoke the fire. The room was already chilly – it was north facing, and always got the brunt of the winds and the storms. Quickly, Mary arranged the firewood in the fireplace, with some crumpled up newspaper and kindling added at the bottom of the pile so that a merry blaze would get going more quickly.

She lit the fire and spent a few minutes with the bellows and the poker, blowing it and poking it and encouraging that blaze as hot as it would go. She was a natural when it came to fires, and she guessed it was a mixture of having patience and a knack for knowing when to step in.

Hopefully, the same qualities would help her now, at this crucial stage of the investigation.

Although her main focus was on the fire, Mary found herself checking over her shoulder every minute or two. Crouched down, with all her attention on making a fire, left her in a vulnerable position.

Someone could sneak up behind her and… thwack.

No doubt, Inspector Braham would be called in to say she must have bumped her head accidentally on the top of the fireplace, Mary thought angrily.

After the fire was blazing, making the room warmer by the minute, she walked around the room and closed the curtains that covered the large bay windows – three in total. The curtains were a deep, forest green in color, which paired well with the pale brown carpet and the furniture, whose upholstery was a mixture of green, cream and brown. It made the room feel like a woodland retreat.

She hoped that Gilbert would be safe here, if he came for tea!

With a shiver, Mary remembered that there were poisoners here as well as murderers. This house was infested with criminal intent.

After drawing the curtains, she moved to the tea tray, boiling the kettle, readying the teapot, and making sure that there were enough Shrewsbury biscuits transferred from the large glass jar in the parlor's cupboard, onto the plate with the lace doily that stood by the cups.

And once all that was done, tea was ready, and her chore was done.

She'd hoped that the routine work, automatically done, would free her mind to focus on what she knew so far. But, disappointingly, her brain wasn't offering her any further details.

The only thing her brain was dredging up was a strange memory that Mary knew she didn't need at this time. It was the memory she'd fleetingly thought about while in the bedroom, discussing the case with Gilbert.

And it had been a strange one, that was for certain.

The memory was centered around the aroma of fragrant dry tea, that she'd smelled inside that secret passage, while escaping from Lady Middlefield's bedroom. And that had brought back an encounter that she'd once had with Mr. Watson, a couple of years ago, at the factory where she'd worked.

Now, rolling up her sleeves and giving the parlor a quick, final polish and dust, Mary thought about that conversation.

It had been a cold, wintry day – much like today, in fact, and she'd gone into Mr. Watson's office to ask for some supplies of oil. The machines always needed top-ups on cold days, but he didn't like the oil to be wasted.

"Afternoon, sir. May we have a bottle of oil, please?"

She'd stopped, sniffing curiously, because the small office that was up the steel staircase above the factory floor hadn't smelled as it usually did, of dust and metal and the tobacco from Mr. Watson's pipe.

It had smelled, richly and deliciously, of Earl Grey tea. What a beautiful smell! Mary had breathed it in greedily, because there had been a shortage of tea recently – apparently a delivery had been diverted and a truck's contents had been lost.

Along with milk, sugar and meat, tea had been unavailable for a fortnight, and the girls had been forced to make do with hot water and hot milk as a substitute. In the factory, most workers needed at least three to four cups of tea a day. Not only was it warming, it was also energizing – especially when combined with a dash of milk and a spoon of sugar, neither of which had been available either.

"Oooh, you got hold of some tea, sir?" she asked.

He'd chuckled. "This is special. Not available to everyone." He wrapped his hands around the mug and lifted it to his lips, and Mary watched every move, the way she imagined that a hungry cat must have watched a bird. That tea looked *so* good.

"I got it for a price," he boasted. "Tea, milk and sugar. If you have money, in these times, sometimes one can buy these little luxuries." Then he'd seen her face, and how thirsty she clearly looked, and the way her gaze was following that tea.

"Go on," he said. "I'll let you have a mug of it. Pour yourself one, be my guest. Milk and sugar included – just not more than one spoon, alright? Stuff's darned expensive!"

It was darned unavailable for her. Wishing so badly for a sip of that fragrant brew, Mary had reminded herself it would be unfair for her to enjoy a cuppa, when all the other girls on the factory floor were still going without. Just because she'd been the one to come and ask for oil didn't mean she should get something they couldn't have.

"Actually, although I'm really grateful, I'll say no thank you," she said. "We're running a little behind time this afternoon, with needing the oil. So I'll leave you to enjoy it, if that's alright? And can I please have the oil?"

She needed to get out of there before she weakened. Her self-control was eroding by the minute. Another few moments of standing there and she'd change her mind and beg for the tea after all.

He'd gotten up, and fetched the oil from the locked cupboard behind his desk, and handed it to her, looking relieved that he hadn't had to share his bounty.

And she'd gone back downstairs, her feet clanging on the metal treads, and every fiber of her being longing for a warm, hearty, sugary sip of that deliciously strong looking brew.

She'd never told the other girls about it. Mary had decided that it wouldn't have been wise, with so many shortages, to say that the boss had been enjoying what was basically contraband goods, even though he'd offered her some.

And even to be offered – it might have caused some jealousy. Some resentment, toward her and toward Mr. Watson.

She'd said nothing about it, but that moment of yearning for tea had etched itself in her mind. Now, she was remembering it.

How strange, she thought, to be vividly recalling such a brief, poignant episode at this time.

And then, with a cold shock as her brain caught up, she realized why she'd thought of it. It did add up, and it was relevant, and now, she had figured out the reason.

"Oh, no!" A sense of doom filled Mary as she understood what had really happened at Middlefield Manor during the war.

CHAPTER TWENTY FIVE

"It was war profiteering!" Mary breathed. "That's what they were doing here. Selling off the tea and sugar and milk and meat that should have come to us, and others!"

Colin, the eldest son, had clearly seen that the estate was on the skids, and he'd acted to save it, in a highly illegal way. Somehow, the estate had been used as a hub – diverting, storing and redistributing rationed goods that had been on their way to the cities from the ports, or the farms in the area.

And instead of being transported to the central distribution points to be rationed out to the hungry people who had been going without, and who had their coupons ready for their meager share, they'd been sold for a sky-high price on the black market. These supplies had been diverted and bought by wealthy folk who wanted more tea and more sugar, more milk and meat than the share that the wartime government had allocated them.

No wonder that secret passageway had smelled of tea! It was because tea had been stored there. And other scarce commodities, she was sure, had been stashed away in that now-empty storeroom down the hill from the stables. It had all been part of the same initiative.

Colin had clearly masterminded it. While she'd been telling Gilbert about it, Sarah-Jane must have started to suspect that there had been something untoward going on.

"He is not what he seems."

Colin Middlefield had taken over the estate's black market activities, running them from a secret passage that led out of his bedroom, and from a secluded storeroom that was down the hill from the stable barn.

No wonder he'd been so bad-tempered and defensive. Cheating on his wife hadn't been his only secret. There had been a more serious one – that involved cheating on the entire country! Dealing in rationed goods meant some people profited and others went without. If he hadn't been stashing tea away via illegal conduits, to sell it at a premium, she and the girls and many others might not have had to forego their tea during that awfully long fortnight and over many other days.

But how had he done it? And did anyone else know about it?

Well, there would surely have been no reason to tell Martin, the sickly middle son. And the youngest son, Warwick, was a rake and a spendthrift who hadn't been here much of the time. Definitely not the kind of person you would consider entrusting such a secret to.

Although, remembering that conversation she'd overheard between Colin and Warwick, Mary guessed that he might have known something, but that Colin was harshly reminding him he couldn't tell.

How about Lady Middlefield?

Now, there was a worrying thought. Did the grand dame herself know? Would she have sanctioned such a thing? She went through all the estate's ledgers. Surely she'd have picked something up?

Casting her mind back, remembering what she knew of Lady Middlefield, Mary didn't think she could have known. Surely a woman of such steely self will would not have condoned it?

So it would have been Colin alone. He had known, and when Sarah-Jane had figured it out and confronted him, he'd killed her.

Now she understood the panic she'd heard in her friend's voice. No wonder Sarah-Jane had had no idea what to do, and been scared to talk about it.

Colin was extremely influential, and he'd even bribed the inspector. He wielded a considerable amount of power. He must have had others in the estate helping him, possibly even a couple of the servants, and he must have pulled the wool over his mother's eyes, and shown her false records.

And that meant she, right now, had to take this higher. She would need to confront the grand dame and tell her what had happened. Frankly, that was a terrifying idea. Mary couldn't think of anything that she'd like to do less than that.

At any rate, she had to try. What was the worst that could happen? She could be fired? At least, if she told Lady Middlefield, then nobody would dare to kill her – or to kill Gilbert.

Should she take Hannah with her?

Mary hesitated as she considered that idea, with her feather duster poised in mid-air. Hannah would be a brilliant person for moral support, but if she ended up being fired, she didn't want Hannah to suffer the same consequences. And that was a real possibility if things went bad.

No, all things considered, she needed to do this alone. That way, her friend would be protected, and Hannah would still have a job.

When to do it?

The sooner, the better, Mary decided. The longer she delayed, the more chance there was for whoever had been listening at Gilbert's bedroom door – presumably Colin – to put into action a vindictive plan for revenge, involving both Gilbert and her.

So, that meant… now?

Gulping with nervousness, Mary gave the feather duster one last pass around the corner of the parlor. It was sparkling clean, but chasing down a nonexistent cobweb gave her a moment to collect her thoughts.

It was nearly teatime, and that meant Lady Middlefield might have retired for a nap or a lie down, or to play another game of patience. She'd be on her own in her rooms, and that was where Mary needed to find her.

She set off, detouring only to put her feather duster away.

Then, she headed for the ornate staircase that would lead her up to Lady Middlefield's suite, walking quickly, so she could outrun her fear and get there before she lost her nerve.

Arriving at the white-painted door, she knocked on it politely, feeling like her heart was keeping time with those quick, urgent taps.

There was no reply.

Mary pushed open the door a crack. "Lady Middlefield?" she called.

She wasn't here. She wasn't in her rooms, and that meant she would be – where?

The conservatory. That was the only other option. Maybe she'd gone to that room for some peace and quiet, wanting some time alone after having bade goodbye to all the guests.

That was where she was going, then.

Although – before she went…

Yet another dark suspicion was now occurring to Mary.

The assistant! Howard!

Had he known about this? He also handled a lot of the estate's money matters, and he could have been the conduit between Lady Middlefield and Colin.

Right now, she was within a yard of his office door, and it was closed. He clearly wasn't inside, but all his paperwork would be there, neatly filed away. If she was going to get the chance to look into his affairs, it needed to be now. She wouldn't get a second chance.

And if he had any records of what happened, then there would be proof to show Lady Middlefield. Proof would really help her now.

Mary hesitated only a moment. She was committed to this – she'd gone too far to back out of it. Her secret was that she knew everyone else's now. And she couldn't keep silent about it any longer.

Taking a deep breath, she walked into the office.

As she had expected, it was as neat as could be. Folders, clearly labeled, were stacked in a bookcase. Ledgers with perfectly penned entries were stacked at right angles to the desk. Even the trash can was empty. Not so much as a stray paperclip spoiled the picture.

It made it difficult to know where to start, Mary acknowledged, feeling a surge of nerves that she was actually standing here, in this office, ready to pry into the household's affairs. If she was wrong – there would be so much trouble.

She wasn't wrong, she reminded herself. She couldn't be wrong. This was the only explanation that made sense. All she was doing, was figuring out if Howard knew some of what was going on, or if he was also oblivious to it.

The ledgers would be the best place to start, then. That was where all the household expenses would be listed, and maybe the income, too. If there was anything unexplained, it might be obvious in the entries. In fact, Sarah-Jane might even have come here herself yesterday afternoon, looking for the same evidence that Mary was hoping to find now.

She opened the first ledger and paged back hurriedly, checking the dates, not wanting to spend any longer in this office than she had to.

This one was too recent; it didn't go back far enough. She needed one that went back at least two years. She skipped the next one in the row, and took out the following one, hoping that it would be correct.

Dates. She needed dates, and she needed amounts, and she also needed the ability to work out if any of them were wrong. She hoped she'd be able to do that. Mathematics was not her strong suit. If only she'd had more natural ability for figures.

Feverishly, feeling a sense of urgency bear down on her, she paged back, and then back further.

And then, at last, staring at the columns of figures while her mind raced, she saw something.

There were two identical rows on two consecutive pages. One was all the way at the back of the ledger, and one was on the second to last page.

But the amounts, and the entries, were different.

One was a series of columns that simply showed that farming activities had become more profitable, with the prices of certain commodities rising sharply.

She felt certain this was the page that had been prepared for Lady Middlefield's perusal.

The next page, with identical figures, had different entries, much more brief.

"Goods Received. Goods Dispatched. Goods Stored."

Yes, these brief, cryptic notations pointed the way to what was really going on. And she needed to take this book with her, to show Lady Middlefield. She could conceal it in her clothing, under her apron.

Mary closed the book and eased it under her apron, wishing there was a nice big pocket there. She'd have to hold the book very still and hope that nobody noticed where her hand was.

At least she finally had the proof to convince the lady – and she had the evidence that while Colin had been the main perpetrator, Howard had known about it and had made sure the records were in a fit state for Lady Middlefield to see.

She turned to face the door, and shock pulsed through her.

Howard was standing in the doorway. Neat as a pin in his smart tweed suit, he had his arms folded and a strange look on his face. A look that Mary had never seen there before.

"Well," he said. "It seems that you've stumbled upon something you weren't supposed to know about."

CHAPTER TWENTY SIX

Mary stared at Howard in horror. He'd crept up behind her, silent as a cat, and now she'd been found out. She was too late. And she didn't like that tone in his voice at all. There was something distinctly menacing about it.

"I – I –" There was nothing she could say that would deflect his suspicion. He had obviously been standing here and watching her. He'd seen her flip through the ledger. That must have been when he arrived. The sound of the pages turning had disguised his footsteps.

"You know. You've been sticking your nose into other people's business, haven't you? Just like your friend!"

The note of threat in his voice was clear and sharp.

Now, she was beginning to realize who the brains in charge of the operation had been.

Not Colin, with his quick temper and his abrupt manner.

It was this man, who was far more deviously intelligent, and would have lost his very comfortable job if the estate had gone bankrupt.

"You masterminded it?" she said, appalled.

Howard shrugged. "Somebody had to. It was a countrywide operation, and we played an important part. It paid handsomely. We came out of it rich. Who wouldn't have done such a thing?" Lowering his voice, he continued. "We were brought down by historic debt, and by a wealth tax when the old lord died. He didn't leave the estate in good shape – and then things were difficult in the war, of course. Colin managed well enough, in a limited way, when he wasn't buying horses with the money. Martin had a brain, but was too sick to run things, so we left him out of it. And, of course, Warwick knew nothing of it. He didn't care. All he wanted to do was spend the money! But those dealings got our estate back on its feet. It's a profitable and well-run venture on its own now. All that's in the past. And that is the little secret that I'll do anything to keep."

Mary swallowed hard. She was in a precarious situation now, all the more so since she'd just seen the large steel mallet on the floor by the door. She knew what that had been used for… and what it would be used for.

There was nobody else around, and nobody within shouting distance. The only person likely to hear her was Colin, whose rooms were closest, and he was complicit in this.

She was trapped in the room, with Howard at the door. In a minute, as soon as he'd stopped bragging about his criminal achievements, he was going to grab the mallet and kill her.

Then he'd probably roll her up in the rug, tell Colin to carry her out, and put her body in the carriage house, claiming she must have bumped her head on the same invisible piece of machinery that had killed Sarah-Jane.

First and foremost, Mary needed to get out of this room. Her strategy after that was unclear, to say the least. But being in this room right now, she was trapped and at his mercy.

As if sensing that it was time, he bent down and picked up the mallet, hefting it in his right hand.

"Put down that ledger and come here," he said.

"I'm not going to put it down," she said, gripping the book firmly. It was evidence of hiding criminal activities, and Lady Middlefield needed to see it. "And I'm not coming over there either. It's a lovely invitation," she added, surprised to find herself capable of sarcasm at such a tense time, "but nonetheless I'm going to refuse it."

"Then I'll come to you," he threatened.

What could she do? What could she use? Gazing in a panicked way around the annex, Mary's mind raced as she considered her options.

She didn't have many, and at that tense moment, could only think of one.

Picking up the main ledger that she'd looked through first – the current one – in her other hand, Mary moved to the fireplace. It was burning brightly, and the fire had clearly been stoked earlier in the afternoon in preparation for the chilly storm to come.

"I'm sure it would set your accounting back considerably," Mary threatened, "if I were to throw this book onto the fire? Not the one with all the misdoings in. I'm talking about the one you're using now. You've got quite a lot of entries in here so far. You wouldn't want to redo all of them, would you? You might not even remember some of them. And how would you explain to Lady Middlefield that the book had been destroyed?"

Her instinct was right. With a desperate look on his face, Howard lunged forward.

"I'm not doing all that work again! Don't you dare!"

Mary watched him carefully. The desk was between him and the fireplace. In order to reach her, he'd have to come around the desk. And as soon as he did – she was going to take the only escape route open to her. She was going to run around the other side of the desk and out of the door.

She tensed, waiting. He leaped toward her, coming around the right side of the desk with the mallet raised.

Mary did the two things that she desperately hoped would slow him down for long enough to save her.

She flung the current ledger onto the fire in a shower of sparks.

And then, she hurtled around the left-hand side of the desk, racing for the door as fast as she could go – and still holding the incriminating ledger tightly in her hand.

Behind her, she heard a cry of fury. Then she heard a metallic rattle. That was probably Howard knocking the book out of the flames with the mallet. She didn't think it would be badly damaged from a moment or two in the fire, with its thick, leather-bound cover.

But at least it had slowed him down long enough for her to reach the door. She darted out and headed down the corridor, knowing that she was running for her life.

The rapid thud of footsteps told her that Howard was following.

He was a slim man, but long legged, and in a race, she knew he would catch her fast. Worse still, she didn't dare to shout out for help, because the wrong person might be alerted, and then this chase would be doubly deadly.

She had to get out of this wing of the house! That was going to be her only chance.

Mary raced down the corridor, her mind going as fast as her legs were. She needed to get down to the kitchens, where there would be people who could help her and protect her from this mallet-wielding murderer.

Ahead, the passage branched, but it only led up to more empty bedrooms and she needed to get somewhere where people would be able to help her. So she ignored that branch, and ran on, grasping to recall the geography of this complicated manor, which Howard knew far better than her.

The best route to take would be through the small drawing room. Mary vaguely remembered that it had an interleading door on each side. She could get through the far door, burst into the corridor, fly down it at the speed of a fleeing hare, and then, she would be in the lodge's main passage and she would be safe from him.

She didn't dare delay. His footsteps were closing in. She could hear them getting louder. Skidding around a bend, she almost cannoned into a wall, containing a large tapestry of a surprised looking, red haired soldier who was riding a horse among a volley of descending arrows.

You and me both, she thought, pushing off from the tapestry to give her the purchase to make the turn. But the footsteps were following, and she feared he was gaining on her.

Mary couldn't risk looking around to see how close he was. She had to focus on getting away. A treacherous fold of carpet slipped under her flying feet, and she gasped, nearly falling flat on her face.

Behind her, a triumphant laugh rang out. He thought he had her!

With a superhuman effort, Mary managed to scramble to her feet and find the last burst of speed she needed to take her into the small drawing room.

There was the doorway ahead. The room was empty, as she'd expected, and it was chilly, the fire not even lit. It was one of the many rooms in this enormous lodge that were seldom used. The most traffic it saw were the servants, the housemaids who came in every couple of days, to dust off the deep pink wingback chairs, and the elegant ottoman with its jade green upholstery, and polish the mahogany tables to a blinding shine.

There was the elegant, white-painted, double door at the end – leading to the main corridor, and to a route where she could finally run to get help.

Dodging around the coffee table, with its porcelain bowl filled with potpourri, Mary raced to the double door.

She wrenched it open - and then ricocheted off it, staggering back into the room.

The door was locked.

She was trapped. And Howard was racing into the drawing room, mallet at the ready.

With a cry of triumph, brandishing it high, he rushed toward her.

CHAPTER TWENTY SEVEN

Gasping for breath, Mary turned and rattled the door again in desperation. Locked? She hadn't known it would be! This was a catastrophe, and it had meant the difference between life and death.

With her back to the door and her hands raised, she faced him. The wild gleam in his eyes told her that he wouldn't hold back – but the only chance she now had was to parry as many of these deadly blows as she could, before he finally got in the one that would kill her.

But, as he approached, snorting triumphantly in a way that chilled her blood, Mary heard another sound from beyond the small drawing room's main doorway.

It was *another* sound of frantically running feet.

Somebody else was heading this way. Her stomach twisted as she feared it would be Colin.

But the person who burst into the room, looking as purposeful as she'd done, was not Colin. To her astonishment, she saw it was Barry, the poisoner. He was holding a blue velvet box in his hand and had a furtive glint in his eyes.

"Um, good afternoon," he said, giving Howard a surprised glance. "I just – er – well, I wanted to have a private word with this most excellent housemaid, Mary. I've procured – er – a small gift, just a token of my thanks for your hard work, which I was hoping you'd accept.

Mary didn't know who was the more shocked – herself or Howard, who hastily lowered the mallet, hiding it away in a fold of his coat as Barry sidled toward them, holding the box out, with a big, fake smile on his face.

"Now is not a good time," Howard snapped out. "Get out of here!"

But in his efforts to fulfill his agenda of making sure she didn't talk about the poisoning, Barry was deaf to his pleas.

"It's from my – er – private collection," he said obsequiously. "Thick, yellow gold, and no jewels – well, there's one small diamond, but perhaps you can overlook it?"

Breathless from her run, Mary was struggling to get enough air into her lungs to tell him no – that even in the current circumstances, she wasn't going to accept it.

Before she could, though, there was another sound that got everyone's heads turning in surprise.

More running footsteps, heading toward the small drawing room.

Hannah burst into the room, skirts flying, her lacy cap askew and her brown, curly hair billowing out.

"What's happening?" she gasped. "I saw you people chasing my friend. I'd – er – I'd like to respectfully ask you, sirs, to please move away from her! Now!"

Having done her best to strike a balance between politeness and firmness, Hannah marched across the room, past Barry and Howard, to stand shoulder to shoulder with Mary.

Mary gave her a glance of pure gratitude. What bravery!

"Thank you," she whispered.

"Will you please all leave the room!" Howard's voice was high and stressed. "I need to have a very serious, disciplinary conversation with this housemaid. Alone!"

"No!" Angrily, Barry faced him down. "I need to have that conversation more urgently than you do. Will you please all leave the room so that I can speak to Mary!"

"I'm not leaving!" both Hannah and Howard said at exactly the same time.

And then, to Mary's astonishment, there was yet another sound of running footsteps from outside.

They all swung around once more as Gilbert, wearing hiking boots and a waxed jacket, came charging into the room.

"What's happening here?" he asked. "I was out on a walk when I saw you running past the window, Mary! Is everything alright? Are you in any danger? What on earth's going on?" he asked in surprise, taking in the numbers that were present.

The small drawing room was fuller of people than Mary guessed it had been for years. And at last, she had what she needed – a team of people who could back her up, none of whom was Colin.

It was time to turn the tables.

She took a deep breath. Then she pointed at Howard.

"This man murdered Sarah-Jane!" she announced, in a loud voice, with as much conviction behind the words as she could summon. "And he was chasing me, ready to do the same!"

Everyone swung around and stared at Howard, who was now shifting uneasily from foot to foot.

"I did no such thing! What a ridiculous assumption. You're away with the fairies, that's for sure. Not focusing on your job, like you should be doing!"

"You're still holding the mallet! It's hidden under your jacket!" Mary insisted. Now was the time when she needed – really needed – to sway this her way.

"Under my… good heavens! So it is!"

There was a thud as the mallet dropped to the floor.

"You're a murderer!" Barry shouted, an excited gleam in his eye, which Mary attributed partly to the fact that he'd finally found somebody at Middlefield Manor who'd committed a more serious crime than he'd done himself.

Given that, Barry wasn't going to let Howard get away.

He lunged toward the assistant, and after a fractional pause, horror written all over his face, Howard turned, and darted out of the open door.

"Get him! He's been caught red-handed!" Gilbert shouted.

With a thunder of feet, everyone in the small living room headed for the door, ready to chase down the guilty man who'd been caught with a murder weapon on his person.

Gilbert was first through the door, racing down the corridor, with Barry hot on his heels. Hannah narrowly beat Mary to the doorway, and then they were running neck and neck down the wide passage, with its flagstoned floor and its narrow bay windows.

"Where is he? Which way did he turn?" Gilbert shouted, pausing at the place where the corridor branched in two.

"I don't know!" Barry yelled back.

"You go right, I'll go left?" Without waiting for a reply, Gilbert raced down the left-hand branch of the corridor. That meant Barry veered right – and Mary and Hannah had to make a choice about who to follow.

They might be slower than the men, but sometimes, being slower meant there was more time to look around. And when chasing a fugitive who was extremely sneaky, and familiar with every secret passage and hidden entrance in this manor house, they'd need to keep their eyes peeled.

Mary didn't trust Barry. She knew that Gilbert would put his heart and soul into the chase, but Barry? He might get distracted or give up.

At least one of them needed to follow Barry. And it couldn't be her. If he saw her pounding along behind him, he might forget all about the chase, and start negotiating with her all over again to accept some jewelry in exchange for not mentioning the poisoning.

"You follow Barry," she gasped to Hannah. "Look out for hiding places along the way. Howard knows them all."

She had just time to see Hannah's nod of confirmation, and then they were veering off in their separate directions – she to the left, Hannah to the right – with no clear idea as yet which way the killer might have gone.

But she could not let any potential hiding place slip by.

With Gilbert charging ahead, trying to catch up with the speedy fugitive, Mary made sure to bring up the rear effectively by checking every hiding place where he could have gone.

There was a door to the right. Was this open?

She wrenched at it, but found it locked, and there was no noise coming from the other side. No heavy breathing that might indicate he'd locked it, and was hiding behind it, waiting for them to pass.

The next door was open, and looking in, she saw a spare bedroom, decked out in drapes of sky blue and yellow gold. The luxurious room was empty, but she bent down and checked under the bed just in case.

Then, still hearing the pounding feet now far ahead of her, she sped up, seeing that Gilbert had now reached the end of the corridor. Ahead, was a tall, barred door – that led outside. And the door was ajar.

That meant Howard could well have fled out into the estate's grounds.

With the sun set, and a storm gripping the area, that was a sneaky move, and it might just allow him to escape scot-free.

Speeding up as fast as she could go, Mary raced ahead to the doorway, seeing blustery darkness beyond. As she reached the door, a gust of wind blew it closed so hard it almost knocked her off her feet.

She wrenched it open and raced outside, gasping as a sheet of freezing rain sluiced over her. This was like being under a waterfall. This winter storm was torrential, and the wind from the northeast meant it blew into her face, and not just down onto her already soaked, lacy cap.

Now, more than ever, she needed to keep alert.

Ahead, she heard a shouted word, only just audible over the maelstrom. "Stop! Hey, stop!"

That was Gilbert. And if he was shouting, it must mean that he had Howard in his sights.

Mary sped up, following the source of the sound, that led her on a zigzag route through the rose garden, past a well trimmed bank of lavender, and over a grassy hill.

There, on the other side of the hill, she saw Gilbert, legs flying. And beyond him, now visible and in her sights, she saw the tweed figure, the suit dark with water, pounding resolutely along a paved walkway that curved around to the summer house, and then stretched ahead.

Where was he going? She couldn't outrun him, but she could outthink him. Having erupted out into the stormy night, he must have a plan in mind – so what was it?

With a clench of her heart, Mary thought she knew. The runaway man wasn't seeking out any of the estate's hidden passageways. He had a much bolder idea in mind.

He was heading for the garages.

Once behind the wheel of a car, he'd be able to make a speedy getaway while in the dry.

They had to get there in time to stop him.

CHAPTER TWENTY EIGHT

Was there a quicker route to the garage?

Pausing in the sluicing rain, Mary tried to remember if there were any sneaky shortcuts that could help her. Howard was taking a longer route. Perhaps he was hoping to increase his lead on the way, or else, confuse the people who were chasing him. Gilbert didn't know the estate at all.

That was what he was doing. His headlong dash was going to take him into a knot of thick woods, where several pathways diverged. If he then doubled back, taking the sharp left pathway, he'd have an easy run down to the garage. He could be in a car, and up the driveway, before Gilbert was even out of the woods.

"He's going to the garage! To get a car!" Mary yelled at the top of her voice, hoping that her hunch was correct, and praying that Gilbert would be able to pick up on what she was saying.

She veered left herself now, bypassing the woods, racing straight down to the stone building which she could see ahead of her, through the pouring rain.

Once, it must have been an additional storage area for hay or straw. The building was large and solid, big enough for twenty cars, even though only three or four were parked inside. It was where all the estate vehicles were housed. There was a Bugatti and a Rolls Royce, a Daimler-Benz and a Jaguar.

And she was right. From deep inside the shed, headlights were blazing. He'd been lightning fast, and must have had his keys, and his plan, at the ready. He was going to speed out of the shed and race out of the estate, and then their criminal would be gone. They needed him here!

Mary wanted this dangerous man brought to book before he had the chance to disappear.

But already, the bright headlights of the Daimler Benz, at the back of the building, were wheeling around in her direction. If she tried to stand in front of the car, he'd simply run her down. And Gilbert, who was now flying down the hill toward her, wouldn't get there in time –

and in any case, the ruthless Howard wouldn't hesitate to flatten him like a pancake either!

A gust of wind nearly knocked Mary off her feet – and as she recovered her footing, her heart pounding in desperation, she realized what her only solution was.

The wind! It, and it alone, could help her now.

Leaping to one of the big, wooden barn doors, Mary bent down and dragged away the big wedge of wood that was in place on the paving stones to hold it open.

She dropped the ledger on the ground, and shoved at the door as hard as she could. It was big and heavy, but if she could move it just slightly, then it might be enough.

The headlights were getting brighter. The Daimler-Benz's engine was shrieking as Howard headed for the doorway.

And Gilbert was now charging directly toward the path of the car, putting himself at risk – if her plan didn't work, he stood a big chance of being seriously hurt.

Then, the wind gusted again, violently. It grabbed the big wooden door and blew it so hard that the door swung shut in a moment.

The closing door met the departing car with a massive bang. The door flew back and then, grabbed by the wind again, it was hurled the other way for a second impact with the car.

But the car wasn't going anywhere.

The Daimler-Benz had collided with the door so hard that the hood was crumpled, steam was erupting from the engine, and Howard had sustained a nasty bump on the head from the steering wheel. He was slumped over it, groaning in pain.

Gilbert didn't hesitate. He rushed forward, grabbed the semi-conscious man's arm, and dragged him out of the car. Eager to help, Mary grabbed his other arm. They were both gasping for breath – but now, more footsteps were arriving.

Barry and Hannah burst into the garage. They were followed by the butler, carrying an umbrella and wearing an astounded expression. The housekeeper was hot on his heels. Clearly, their headlong race through the manor had alerted the staff, and now, they were rallying round to help.

"We need to call the police," Gilbert said breathlessly. "This man is a dangerous fugitive. Lock him away until the police arrive!"

"Somewhere that doesn't have a secret passage," Hannah added, firmly.

"Before the police get here, please, I need to do something." Mary finally found enough air to start speaking herself. She bent down and picked up the ledger that contained the all-important evidence she needed, brushing the rain off its cover. "Before the police get here, I need to speak to Lady Middlefield. And I need to do it alone."

CHAPTER TWENTY NINE

"You are certain that all of this is true?"

Lady Middlefield was remaining remarkably calm, Mary thought. It didn't even seem as if the grand dame was shocked by the news. She was the one who felt like a bundle of nerves, uncertain if her version of events would be accepted or believed.

They were sitting in the master bedroom – the lady on her wingback chair, and Mary on a wooden stool. On the desk in between them, the ledger was resting, open at the incriminating page.

"My lady," she said politely, "Howard admitted to the crime of murder. He said he had killed Sarah-Jane because she found out the truth – which, as you can see, is recorded in this ledger."

"And he did it along with Colin?"

"Yes, my lady. Not the murder – that, Howard did alone. But the other crime – war profiteering – that crime, they were in on together. They stored the items in the secret passageway between your rooms and Colin's rooms, and also in the store room down the hill from the stables."

"A very serious offense." Lady Middlefield sounded stern. "Never would I have condoned such behavior, but it was kept from me in a very devious way."

"Unfortunately, there are a lot of secrets that were circulating here in this manor," Mary said.

She realized, too late, that it had been unwise to say that. Because, fixing her with a steely gaze over her spectacles, Lady Middlefield demanded, "Is that so? Well, then, you had better tell me all about them. I don't want anything – and I mean anything – kept from me now."

Mary bit her lip.

"Well, um, there has been some rather unfortunate goings-on between Barry, your cousin, and Martin."

"And what, exactly, occurred?" Lady Middlefield's voice was like a knife.

“You see, there’s this clause in the will, a very minor clause, stating that if your second son is not in good health, then certain properties will go to a cousin instead.”

“Yes, I changed that the year before last, when I cut Warwick out of the will, due to all his goings-on,” Lady Middlefield admitted.

“Unfortunately, it seems that Barry has been trying to create the ill health, by feeding small amounts of arsenic to Martin. I caught him in the act,” Mary admitted.

Now, at last, Lady Middlefield looked appalled.

“I will delete that clause in the will immediately!” she said. “I always believed Martin to be the most intelligent of my sons, and the one best suited to running the estate. But he had an unfortunate fall from a horse which left him poorly for years, and just as he was recovering, these other problems began.” She tapped a nail thoughtfully on the table. “He would be the most responsible heir for the estate when his health improves. Especially if Colin is in prison for war crimes,” she added, not sounding particularly sorry about the idea.

"I'm sure Barry's wife will be devastated, though. Should he go into prison for a long spell?" she said, regarding Mary with a look that told her she might already have guessed that she wouldn't be.

“Possibly, my lady. But in my travels around this manor house, it did come to my attention that – er – that both partners in that marriage were having affairs, or at any rate, romantic moments, with others," she admitted.

This was like being questioned by the Spanish Inquisition.

“Give me names,” the lady demanded.

Nothing for it. She’d have to say. Keeping silent was not an option now.

“Well, I saw Colin and Lady Ainsley together,” she admitted. “And Colin’s wife – she was, er, having a tender moment with Warwick, which I heard about. But you see, Warwick is in financial difficulty. He owes people a lot of money, and he – he’s been trying to get that money by stealing your things. The elephant, and your golden necklace. They’re both hidden away in his mattress, on the headboard side.”

She could see that wasn’t good news. The grand dame’s lips tightened.

“This is extremely disturbing.”

“I’m very sorry to have to be the bearer of such bad news.”

“Finding my ornamental elephant is not bad news,” the lady corrected her. “I will decide how to handle all of this in due course,” she said. "For now, I can see in your eyes that this isn't all. What else have you discovered?"

But Mary shook her head.

There was one secret that she wasn't going to repeat under any circumstances, and that was Gilbert's. It had been told to her in confidence and trust, and it didn't affect any of the people at Middlefield Manor, because he was a guest, and not family at all.

"That's all, my lady," she said firmly.

Lady Middlefield's gaze was like a dagger.

"I don't believe you."

"As long as you believe everything else I've said, then I think we've reached the end of this conversation," Mary said politely.

"Tell me!" the lady pressured her again, her voice intense, but Mary shook her head.

"No, my lady. I've told you everything relevant."

"But not everything there is!" She sounded as mad as a wet hen not to have been let in on the remaining secret, but Mary wasn't going to budge.

After a short, furious silence, the lady continued.

"Well. You have certainly caused ructions during your brief tenure with us. And you have proven to me that you are not entirely loyal." That unspoken secret was really gnawing at her. It seemed that the lady was by way of being rather a gossip.

She continued, with a voice like ice. "With that in mind, I have decided what my next step will be – not involving the family. But involving you."

CHAPTER THIRTY

By the time Mary reeled out of Lady Middlefield's private boudoir, the manor house was in a state of chaos. The police had arrived. Inspector Braham was back – together with one junior constable, and one stern, gray haired officer who appeared to be his senior.

As she passed the hallway, where both Howard and Colin were standing in handcuffs, flanked by two footmen and Mrs. Inglethorpe, she heard Inspector Braham's voice, loud and confident as he addressed his boss.

"I was able to uncover new information, which convinced me that this crime was not a simple accident but something far more nefarious, sir!"

Mary felt like rolling her eyes. If only that loose end had been wrapped up to her satisfaction – but it hadn't, and the devious constable had managed to cover his back.

Still, that was a minor concern compared to the very serious predicament she now found herself in.

Hoping that Hannah would have retreated to the staff pantry by now, after such an exhausting conclusion to a long working day, Mary headed that way, turning down the corridor that led to the kitchen. Her heart felt heavy with the burden of the bad news she was going to have to tell her friend and fellow worker.

She was to blame for this, and loyal Hannah was suffering the brunt of it.

But before she even reached the kitchen, she saw Gilbert approaching.

The skip of her heart on seeing him was followed by a plummet of her spirits. It was wonderful to see him this final time, but she had no idea if she'd ever see him again. What a chase that had been, she remembered, doing her best to remind herself of the good times.

"Mary! I've been looking for you. I'm about to leave, but I wasn't going to go without – without saying goodbye, and also telling you something important," he said.

Something important? Wondering what that could be, Mary updated him on her recent activities

“I was in a long interview with Lady Middlefield,” she admitted. “I had to tell her what was going on, and she ended up demanding that I reveal every secret I’ve learned since I’ve been here.”

A mixture of anxiety and concern darkened Gilbert’s face.

"I totally understand the situation, Mary. There was nothing you could do about it if you had to tell her everything."

“I told her everything – except one.” She tapped her chest. “Your secret is safe with me, Gilbert.”

Intentionally, she addressed him by his first name, for the very first time.

Now, gratitude and relief replaced the worry in Gilbert’s eyes as he whispered, “Thank you.”

Mary was willing to leave it there, and in fact, she would have. She had her pride and didn't want to make her problems his.

But when he asked her, in concerned tones, “Tell me truthfully – was there any backlash or consequences to you, because of all of this?” she had no option but to explain.

"Actually, I've been dismissed. And Hannah, too. Lady Middlefield has let us go with a month's extra wages to tide us over while we look for something else, and she'll give us references, but she says she doesn't want us here anymore. I think it would be awkward after – well, after everything that's happened. And she was a bit angry at me for not telling her everything – not that I want you to feel bad about it," she added hurriedly, seeing his face tauten yet again.

She felt sad to burden Gilbert with this, and devastated to be jobless again. And a tiny part of her was wishing that she and Hannah would have had the chance to travel to Skegness and see the sea. But that would never happen now. Viewing the sea was a dream for another day.

“I’m so sorry about that, and I think it’s extremely unfair. But that’s actually what I wanted to discuss with you,” Gilbert said. “I was on the phone with my mother earlier, telling her all about this, and she was most admiring of your actions.”

“Was she?” Mary felt cheered by that.

“She immediately said that if you and your friend were fired, which she suspected might happen, I must tell you that Haversham Hall, which is in Derbyshire, is looking for four new housemaids, as they've just refurbished a whole new wing, and they'd be very glad to take you on, seeing I know you and there's a personal connection." He hesitated, looking at her expectantly. "They're family friends and I travel there regularly – I know it's a decent place to work. Although, I'm not sure what secrets they have," he added with a wry smile.

Mary hesitated for only a moment.

This offer was a godsend, arriving at exactly the right time. And it would mean she'd be able to go to Hannah with good news, instead of landing disaster on her poor friend's shoulders.

She stared Gilbert in the eye, meeting his deep blue gaze, and realizing that after being through all of this together, and learning so much more about him, she felt much closer to him. They felt like they had a deeper connection that hadn't been there before.

Very good friends – but with a spark.

"I'd love to accept that offer on behalf of both of us, as soon as possible," she said. "And if they have any secrets – well, I'll do my best to make sure they stay hidden."

NOW AVAILABLE!

THE MAID AND THE MANSION: A MISSING GUEST
(The Maid and the Mansion Cozy Mystery—Book 3)

In post-World War II England, a clever, young woman named Mary Adams finds herself thrust into a world of privilege and secrets as she transitions from being a wartime factory worker to a maid in the grand estates. As Mary begins a new position in the kitchens of a prestigious family, she finds herself in the midst of an engagement party where the air is thick with tension and secrets. When a poison-induced murder disrupts the façade of a forced union, Mary must uncover the identity of the killer before the killer destroys more than just the engagement….

"Very entertaining. I highly recommend this book to the permanent library of any reader that appreciates a very well written mystery, with some twists and an intelligent plot. You will not be disappointed. Excellent way to spend a cold weekend!"
--Books and Movie Reviews, Roberto Mattos (regarding *Murder in the Manor*)

THE MAID AND THE MANSION: A MISSING GUEST is book #3 in a charming historical cozy mystery series by Fiona Grace, #1 bestselling author of *Murder in the Manor*, which has over 10,000 five star reviews!

As Mary navigates the delicate intricacies of high society, she also finds herself privy to their darkest secrets. As a maid, Mary moves through mansions unnoticed and unheeded, allowing her to overhear tales of jilted lovers, gossip from fellow maids, and secrets straight from the mouths of the rich and elite.

As Mary delves deeper into the intricate web of secrets within the stately manor, she encounters a cast of eccentric and intriguing characters, each with their own secrets—and their own motives for murder.

Will Mary uncover their secrets in time? Or become just another story whispered about in the grand halls?

A charming historical cozy mystery series that transports readers back in time, THE MAID AND THE MANSION is mystery at its finest: spellbinding, atmospheric and impossible to put down. A page-turner packed with shocking twists, turns and a mystery that's hard to solve, it will leave you reading late into the night, all while you fall in love with its unforgettable heroine.

Future books in the series are now available!

"The story line wasn't just a who done it, but had a story about her life and romance, including village life. Very entertaining."
--Reader reviewer (regarding *Murder in the Manor*)

"It has endearing and sometimes quirky characters, a plot that keeps you reading and the right amount of romance. I can't wait to start book two!"
--Reader reviewer (regarding *Murder in the Manor*)

"What a great story of murder, romance, new beginnings, love, friend ships and a wonderful cascade of mystery."
--Reader reviewer (regarding *Murder in the Manor*)

"This is a clean contemporary romance that you will find hard to put down!"
--Reader reviewer (regarding *Always, Forever*)

"A bit of romance and a very determined woman! I have read many of Fiona Grace's novels and loved every one of them—this was no exception. I am looking forward to reading the rest of this new series!"
--Reader reviewer (regarding *Always, With You*)

Fiona Grace

Fiona Grace is author of the LACEY DOYLE COZY MYSTERY series, comprising nine books; of the TUSCAN VINEYARD COZY MYSTERY series, comprising seven books; of the DUBIOUS WITCH COZY MYSTERY series, comprising three books; of the BEACHFRONT BAKERY COZY MYSTERY series, comprising six books; of the CATS AND DOGS COZY MYSTERY series, comprising nine books; of the ELIZA MONTAGU COZY MYSTERY series, comprising nine books (and counting); of the ENDLESS HARBOR ROMANTIC COMEDY series, comprising nine books (and counting); of the INN AT DUNE ISLAND ROMANTIC COMEDY series, comprising five books (and counting); of the INN BY THE SEA ROMANTIC COMEDY series, comprising five books (and counting); and of the MAID AND THE MANSION COZY MYSTERY series, comprising five books (and counting).

Fiona would love to hear from you, so please visit www.fionagraceauthor.com to receive free ebooks, hear the latest news, and stay in touch.

BOOKS BY FIONA GRACE

THE MAID AND THE MANSION COZY MYSTERY

A MYSTERIOUS MURDER (Book #1)
A SCANDALOUS DEATH (Book #2)
A MISSING GUEST (Book #3)
AN UNSOLVABLE CRIME (Book #4)
AN IMPOSSIBLE HEIST (Book #5)

INN BY THE SEA ROMANTIC COMEDY

A NEW LOVE (Book #1)
A NEW CHANCE (Book #2)
A NEW HOME (Book #3)
A NEW LIFE (Book #4)
A NEW ME (Book #5)

THE INN AT DUNE ISLAND ROMANTIC COMEDY

A CHANCE LOVE (Book #1)
A CHANCE FALL (Book #2)
A CHANCE ROMANCE (Book #3)
A CHANCE CHRISTMAS (Book #4)
A CHANCE ENGAGEMENT (Book #5)

ENDLESS HARBOR ROMANTIC COMEDY

ALWAYS, WITH YOU (Book #1)
ALWAYS, FOREVER (Book #2)
ALWAYS, PLUS ONE (Book #3)
ALWAYS, TOGETHER (Book #4)
ALWAYS, LIKE THIS (Book #5)
ALWAYS, FATED (Book #6)
ALWAYS, FOR LOVE (Book #7)
ALWAYS, JUST US (Book #8)
ALWAYS, IN LOVE (Book #9)

ELIZA MONTAGU COZY MYSTERY

MURDER AT THE HEDGEROW (Book #1)
A DALLOP OF DEATH (Book #2)
CALAMITY AT THE BALL (Book #3)

A SPEAKEASY DEMISE (Book #4)
A FLAPPER FATALITY (Book #5)
BUMPED BY A DAME (Book #6)
A DOLL'S DEBACLE (Book #7)
A FELLA'S RUIN (Book #8)
A GAL'S OFFING (Book #9)

LACEY DOYLE COZY MYSTERY
MURDER IN THE MANOR (Book#1)
DEATH AND A DOG (Book #2)
CRIME IN THE CAFE (Book #3)
VEXED ON A VISIT (Book #4)
KILLED WITH A KISS (Book #5)
PERISHED BY A PAINTING (Book #6)
SILENCED BY A SPELL (Book #7)
FRAMED BY A FORGERY (Book #8)
CATASTROPHE IN A CLOISTER (Book #9)

TUSCAN VINEYARD COZY MYSTERY
AGED FOR MURDER (Book #1)
AGED FOR DEATH (Book #2)
AGED FOR MAYHEM (Book #3)
AGED FOR SEDUCTION (Book #4)
AGED FOR VENGEANCE (Book #5)
AGED FOR ACRIMONY (Book #6)
AGED FOR MALICE (Book #7)

DUBIOUS WITCH COZY MYSTERY
SKEPTIC IN SALEM: AN EPISODE OF MURDER (Book #1)
SKEPTIC IN SALEM: AN EPISODE OF CRIME (Book #2)
SKEPTIC IN SALEM: AN EPISODE OF DEATH (Book #3)

BEACHFRONT BAKERY COZY MYSTERY
BEACHFRONT BAKERY: A KILLER CUPCAKE (Book #1)
BEACHFRONT BAKERY: A MURDEROUS MACARON (Book #2)
BEACHFRONT BAKERY: A PERILOUS CAKE POP (Book #3)
BEACHFRONT BAKERY: A DEADLY DANISH (Book #4)
BEACHFRONT BAKERY: A TREACHEROUS TART (Book #5)
BEACHFRONT BAKERY: A CALAMITOUS COOKIE (Book #6)

CATS AND DOGS COZY MYSTERY

A VILLA IN SICILY: OLIVE OIL AND MURDER (Book #1)
A VILLA IN SICILY: FIGS AND A CADAVER (Book #2)
A VILLA IN SICILY: VINO AND DEATH (Book #3)
A VILLA IN SICILY: CAPERS AND CALAMITY (Book #4)
A VILLA IN SICILY: ORANGE GROVES AND VENGEANCE (Book #5)
A VILLA IN SICILY: CANNOLI AND A CASUALTY (Book #6)

Made in the USA
Las Vegas, NV
16 January 2024

84461257R00090